MURDER ON A TWO LANE ROAD

Palamabron Publishing
1916 Pike Place
Suite 12-413
Seattle, WA 98101
206 329 4401

Library of Congress Control Number: 2012938535

ISBN-13(paperback): 978-0-9852264-0-4
ISBN-10(paperback): 0985226404

DIS IS DA DISCLAIMER

Just to make this point very clear, so we can get on to a story that I like a lot, this is a work of fiction. There are real places mentioned in this book, places you can visit and have a lot of fun at. Bars, brothels and strip clubs I have had a great time at and I hope you do, too. But the hijinks and goings on that take place in this book, all came out of my fevered imagination, or my ass, depending on whose opinion you listen to. And the same thing goes for the people in this book, many of them very close friends that I have gleefully maligned. Turning them into bloody handed killers, hookers or even law enforcement officers.

Most of them have been warned, but if I missed some of you, please take your caricature-assassination in good fun and do not get your knickers in any sort of strange configuration.

Onward

Acknowledgements

Many people helped me create this book, my first published mystery thriller.

Let me start with my editors-publishers-managers and great friends, Wally and Belva Lane. Their enthusiastic support and constructive criticism many times got me back to my two-fingered typing on this old computer.

Next comes my muse and confidante, Kate Wyatt. whom I can always count on for a great meal, a sympathetic ear and swift kick in the ass if my ego starts to get too inflated.

Mathew Goossen continues as a stalwart friend and great supporter from his Leschi aerie. Editing and hugs were also accomplished well by Rosalie Mobley, quit often across the bar from Monica McCrea.

Pearl Cline was a great final editor, with her back ground in both English literature and dramatic writing. Despite the fact that she couldn't understand how she would have anything to do with such a smutty book.

Julia Lacquement came through with what I think is a brilliant cover art piece. I wanted it to invoke memories of classic Spillane, Chandler and McDonald. I'm not saying that the book is as good as one of theirs, but I've wanted to write a book like this since I was about twelve years old. I'm glad I finally got to.

This book is a complete work of fiction created wholly in my own twisted mind. The reason I have to stress that is because

I have shamelessly used my friends and acquaintances likenesses and in many cases physical attributes to populate my book; while putting my words in their mouths and turning wonderful, happy, morally-upright human beings into trollops, hookers and in some cases homicidal sociopaths. They bear no responsibility for the actions of these characters. I hope they get a kick out of their metamorphosis.

In a similar manner I have used many actual locations, bars, brothels, strip clubs, restaurants and motels, et cetera, as settings for the action. Once again, the people that live and work in these locations bear no responsibility for what takes place in this book.

The one exception is Angus, the protagonist, who is not nearly so smart, handsome, strong, witty or well hung as the author.

. . .

MURDER ON A TWO LANE ROAD

By

ANGUS VIEIRA

CHAPTER ONE

I woke up with my face buried in a purple silk pillow that smelled of rum, sex and some floral perfume. Small wispy snores came from somewhere near my right ear.

I carefully rolled over, as the confusion in my morning head began to clear.

Matching sheets?

I don't usually get to fuck or even sleep on matching purple sheets.

Stormy was next to me, on her back with her large, perfectly symmetrical, after-market tits rising and falling gently as she slept, and while I'm not a big fan of large implanted breasts, if you are in Stormy's line of work, they up your earnings considerably.

Last night was pretty much back in my memory bank by now, everything but Stormy's real name. So I slipped out of the king-sized bed and caught my foot in my leather jacket on the   floor next to the bed. There was a check for five hundred bucks from Amanda Smith, aka Stormy, in the pocket.

"Thank you, Stormy."

Dressing quickly because I could shower and shave later in my own sleazy motel unit up north, I returned to Stormy's side of the bed and looked down on her. With or without the new tits, she's a treat to look at, whether sleeping with her mouth a little open or swinging around a pole with her ankle by her ear.

She had a tiny patch of pubic hair, kind of a "Hitler mustache" just above her cleft. No other hair down there—totally smooth. When I was finished with my moment of voyeurism, she rolled over. I had to stick around for a second—not a single hair peeked out of her butt crack.

Laser? Or wax? Got to be an interesting job.

I gave her a little nip on her left buttock cheek. She grunted, farted and rolled back over throwing an arm over her eyes.

"Oops," she said.

Amanda had done a lot more damage to that old rum bottle than I had last night.

"Not to worry, I think that's kinda cute. I gotta go, but I wanted to say thanks before I did. Glad I could solve your problem. Tell all your friends," I said.

"Okay, sweetie, thanks for the help and the good time, too, you little stud muffin. This will help me nail that prick's balls to the wall."

A mixed metaphor with a graphic image.

"Come to the club tonight," she said. "It's amateur night. We'll have a giggle watching the new fish."

Amanda waved and spread her legs, giving me a grin and a little burlesque hump.

"You have no shame. I like that in a girl. I might see you later," I said.

Amanda lived in a fine old apartment house near Broadway on Capitol Hill, so I had to park Rooby, my red Buick convertible and constant companion, a couple of blocks away.

Since I was in this part of town, and was generally unable to resist temptation, I stopped for breakfast at Dick's Deluxe Hamburger Stand and then went to the bank next door and deposited Amanda's check, hoping that would stop the whimpering coming from my bank account.

Amanda had not paid me $500 for being a stud muffin. That part was a bonus for getting some photos of her soon-to-be-divorced dentist (The Prick) husband in some explicit sexual hanky-panky with a very sexy Eurasian dancer whom I had set him up with.

Admittedly, that was kind of entrapment and a dirty trick.

My morals are a trifle situational, but I try not to fuck over anyone who didn't deserve it. He deserved it.

I jumped into Rooby and drove through downtown Seattle, headed north on Aurora, out past Greenlake, finally reaching my destination, the Orion Motel, where I washed Amanda out of my mustache.

Around eight that evening I started to feel restless and a little horny again. I remembered what Amanda had said about amateur night at the Déjà Vu topless club.

Money in the bank and I hadn't seen a naked woman in several hours, so I headed Rooby back downtown.

I parked in the Pike Street Market and headed for the Athenian for a couple of cold Pabst Blue Ribbon beers before crossing First Avenue to the strip club.

You see, Washington State could be very tight-assed when it came to "sinful activities" and the Washington State Liquor Control Board was among the tightest. So the nude dancing clubs had gone soda pop several years back, eliminating that little problem.

I perched on a barstool and nodded to Gordy, the bartender. He knows what I drink, so I just spun around and looked out the picture windows at Puget Sound, a hundred and fifty feet down the steep hillside.

A ferry was headed for Colman dock. I never get tired of that view. I do love this city.

I knew that the amateur dancing contest got started around ten o'clock. So a little after nine, I finished my Pabst and was getting ready to saunter across the street, when a very pretty girl wearing a bright red wig perched on the stool next to me.

High tight butt under a miniskirt. Medium sized shapely breasts that did not need, and currently were not encumbered by, a bra, just a blue halter top.

I decided to have another beer.

I was on the backside of forty, turning grey, long ponytail, and in spite of what Stormy said, I don't consider myself every girl's stud muffin. So I don't generally try to pick up twenty-something beauties in waterfront bars. Besides, I was headed to where I knew there would be twenty-something beautiful and naked women.

I wasn't really expecting anything as I gave the lady a smile and nod.

She smiled and nodded back. And then, to my surprise, put her hand on my thigh, looked me in the eye and said, "You look like someone who might be willing to do me a favor. Do you have any special plans for the next couple of hours?"

I shook my head and shrugged, deciding not to mention the strip club, which is why her next question startled me.

"Have you ever been to the Déjà Vu, across the street?"

"As a matter of fact I have."

"I thought you might've. Long hair, no wedding ring and you look like you've been around the block a couple of times."

I ordered another beer.

"Well," she continued, "here's the deal. I plan to go there in a little while and enter the amateur contest. And I want to win, because I can use the two hundred bucks."

I nodded and asked, "Where do I come in?"

"You go over ahead of me." She dug in her purse and pulled out a gaudy card with a sultry nude dancer on it. "I have a free pass to get you in. You have to buy a drink for ten bucks, but other than that you don't have to spend any money. All I ask is that if they pick you as a judge in the contest, you vote for me. Whether I win or lose I'll buy you a drink at the Noc Noc Bar after the contest. Either way, you get to see me naked, if that appeals to you. What do you think?"

Fifteen minutes later I was sitting in front of the stage watching Stormy shuck her G-string and throw it at my head.

I laughed, threw her a dollar and sniffed her crotch. The panty crotch, I mean—I'd already done the other one that day. Not that I'd mind doing it again.

Stormy put her hand over her mouth and widened her eyes in an effort to look shocked, but it didn't work very well because she was thrusting that little Nazi mustache at me over and over while her little pink nipples made small circles in different directions.

That little curly patch south of her belly button was a lot darker brown than the tawny hair that fell past her shoulders. Shocking, huh?

Stormy dropped onto her back and spread her legs very wide, pointing her toes at the ceiling.

I could almost see what she had for breakfast.

She did a backward somersault, landing in a full split.

I painfully envisioned myself doing this, and splitting in two pieces. *Ouch*!

She leaped at the lucky chrome pole at the corner of the stage and for the rest of her number seemed to suspend gravity as she writhed up and down the pole like some agitated tan and pink python. When the song ended, I clapped loudly. Almost no one else did, some of them pretending they had no idea how they ended up in a strip club. I was also the only one to throw Stormy a dollar.

Most American men and women deserve each other. Sometimes it's hard to believe I come from this tight-assed country.

She bounced into the chair next to me grabbing her panties and slapping my knee.

"You are unbelievably naughty. Thanks for the buck anyway. It's nice to know somebody was watching me work my naked ass off. Are you interested in spending some of my money, letting me make your lap all bulgy?"

"Not tonight darlin', I think I'll just watch the amateurs and make an early night of it."

She pulled her panties up and bent over in front of me. The string did not quite cover the pinkish brown wrinkles around her butt hole. So I covered them with my thumb.

She gave a little squeal, turned around and shook her finger at me. "You are so bad. One of these days you'll get me fired, or yourself beat up."

"You are much too sweet to fire and I am way too cute to beat up."

She got a far-off look for a minute. "Nobody's too cute to get beat up."

Then she was back in 'working-girl flirt.' "If they make you a judge, vote for the girl in the red wig, she's a friend of mine."

Interesting. The girl I met at the Athenian was a friend of my client and fuck buddy, Stormy. My antennae twitched a little, but it really wasn't that much of a coincidence. Erotic dancers are kind of a small tribe and a lot of them are bisexual. So they tend to meet and recruit other sexy girls that often need money and don't mind making a bunch of it in their underpants.

I come by my skepticism legitimately, starting with four years in the Marines and my first war, both of which didn't help my trust level in my fellow man. That experience also taught me that life is too short to go through it wearing a uniform and marching around a big parking lot.

Next came my many years as a Marine Engineer, traveling the world's seas and using the world's whorehouses as my social clubs, dating services, and living room.

It took a long time for me to burn out on that one. The money was good, the world had got a lot of very interesting places, and the girls treated me like a rock star.

Then AIDS came along and even the third world girls got fearful of stranger-sex. And the world got a lot more homogenized. Orchard Road in Singapore is now one American fast food chain after another. And I'm trying to write saleable poetry (an oxymoron) and doing some private investigation work. I have a couple of lawyers who use me, and the word got around. I've seen quite a little perfidious human activity and while I still love watching beautiful women I don't always trust them right away.

The girl that came on next was slender, freckled, and a true redhead. She was followed by a beautifully exotic Eurasian, showing off her goodies like they were rare gems. I agreed with her.

While the exotic Eurasian was on stage a large fellow in a suit coat came up to my table and asked if I could assume the great burden of amateur contest judge. It came with a free pass for my next visit and a free porno DVD. A tough job, but I was up for it.

The announcer with the smarmy voice was perfect for the job. He said, "All right guys, here they come. We got four hot amateurs for you here tonight. These sexy girls are vying for your applause and $200 dollars in prize money. So let's welcome the first contestant. She's a twenty-two year old waitress from Renton who calls herself Sweetheart. Let's give her a warm welcome."

Sweetheart had picked the Johnny Cash song about a ring of fire. I've always thought of it as the hemorrhoid song. She was a cute brunette, a little chubby, maybe, but very energetic, probably with a high school cheerleader background.

Her blouse came off over her head and a pink bra followed quickly. She was proud of her pink-tipped B-cups. Then she turned and pulled off her cutoffs, leaving black bikini panties which she pulled down about halfway, wiggling her ass. And that was it.

The big manager had given me a sheet with the girls' names. I gave Sweetheart a seven.

A girl named Ginger was next. If she wasn't a stripper now, she sure had been one some time. Ginger was probably thirty-five, with cat eyes tattooed on either side of her spine, just above her buttocks. She had no problem with nudity; in front of an audience she bent over until her blonde hair touched the stage and peeled down her G-string. She got an 8 from me.

Next out was a pretty young black girl calling herself Mocha. She was obviously a real amateur, nervous and more than a little shy. Like maybe she had a boyfriend in the audience who had egged her on. She only got down to her bra and ruffle-butt pink panties by the end of a slightly annoying rap song. She got a six for showing up.

The announcer said, "All right, we've seen some sexy ladies so far but we sure ain't done yet, let's give it up for Salome."

Stormy gave a rebel yell from the other side of the room.

To the strains of "Beautiful Loser," the girl in the red wig came twirling on stage. She was wearing her halter top and a pair of tiny purple lace panties. You could tell she had probably had some ballet lessons in her past. She whirled her top off and was the first contestant to try the pole, which she swung around on a little awkwardly but at least she gave it a shot. At the end of the song, she too, bent as far over as she could and whipped down the lacy wisp of purple panties.

I am something of a connoisseur of the female ass. It's a hobby. This one was pretty near perfect—high and tight, with just enough downy hair between her cheeks to verify her humanity. I caught just a flash of pink and then she was upright again undulating around the stage.

When the song ended the applause was enthusiastic, with Amanda and me probably being the most energetic.

I wasn't fudging as I gave Salome a ten.

She smiled and waved her arm as she left the stage. I noticed the intricate tattoo on her right forearm.

She won the contest and was called back up to the stage for a last round of applause and ten crisp twenty dollar bills.

I watched one more Oriental "pro" and then left, giving Stormy a pat on the butt as I passed by. I headed across Second Avenue to the Noc Noc, hoping but not necessarily believing that Salome would show up for a drink. I didn't care who bought it.

I like women. You might have figured that out by now.

The Noc Noc is a long bar with two rooms; there's a stage in the second room. The joint's decorated in what I call "Seattle Goth." A large metal winged figure that I found menacingly appealing hung above the bar.

They sold forty-ounce bottles of PBR here for cheap. May Bacchus smile upon them and give them much prosperity.

They also had a burlesque night. Obviously they had their priorities on straight.

I got a big brown bottle and a glass and settled in at the bar. Whether or not the lady showed up, it was a win-win situation.

Ten minutes later she came in and sat next to me, giving my butt a swat as she sat down to the visible disappointment of several men she had passed by to get to me.

She was back in her lucky blue halter-top and black mini skirt with, I imagined, those little purple lace panties snuggled back up where they belonged.

"I won!" she said. "Thanks for your help. Did you pay for that beer? 'Cause I'm buying."

"You can buy the next one if you stay that long. I did vote for you, and I am very happy you won. But I don't think you really needed my help. Either way it was a pleasure seeing your pretty pooper. If you like PBR you can help me with this one."

She had a wide bright smile and a good laugh—not a giggler. Good.

I was starting to like this lady. She had kept her word and had a sense of humor. Two essential qualities if you are going to hang out with me.

"Sure, give me a glass," she said. "I love PBR."

She was making points right and left.

"So although it's a great dancer name, do I have to keep on calling you Salome?"

Again the grin—just a little wild.

"I'm Kate, and you're Angus. Amanda—Stormy—told me when I told her I had a secret accomplice."

She and I finished that 40-ounce bottle thirstily and, true to her word, she bought another one.

"How do you happen to know Amanda?" I asked.

"My father owns a whole bunch of stuff, including a big old bar down in Pioneer Square. A lot of the girls hang out there. They dig the local bands and sometimes there's a pole dancer contest." Then she changed the subject and said, "What about you? What do you do?"

"I'm spending the summer at my favorite nudist camp, writing a book of poetry."

She expressed interest in coming out there some sunny day. I expressed interest in having her come out there and gave her my card.

She said, "I see some smoky treats in your pocket. Let's go out front to the patio and have one. There's a bouncer here I like to flirt with."

We headed out there with our beers and lit up a couple of my Marlboros.

Kate smiled at a fit-looking young guy in a white Honey Tongue T-shirt and gave him a finger wave.

"What does the tattoo on your arm signify?" I asked.

"It's four linked initials, JRRT for Tolkien. I love *The Lord of the Rings* and everything I can read about Middle Earth. There's a lot of books out there."

This lady was turning out to be very interesting.

We sat at one of the tiny wrought-iron tables on the small patio. She asked for another cigarette and I handed it to her just as her friend the bouncer came up behind her and rubbed her neck.

She dropped the smoke between my feet. "Brian, you startled me," she said. She bent down to get the cigarette, putting her head between my knees. A wiseass comment sprang to my lips but I never got it out. Things went sideways in a New York second.

I heard three popping sounds that I knew were gunshots.

They say you don't hear the one that gets you, and I know that's true from personal experience. But you sure do hear the one that goes right by your ear.

I saw two red holes blossom in Brian's white T-shirt and the plate-glass window behind him shattered in a screaming cascade of broken glass.

I closed my knees around Kate's head and threw myself sideways off the chair behind a wooden planter that separated the patio from the street. Kate came with me, of course. I didn't have time to be a gentleman about it.

From the sidewalk I looked at Brian the bouncer, who was slumped against the front door, already looking very dead, times two. From the look on his face, he never heard either one.

Kate looked okay.

I yelled, "Stay down!" then started sneaking along the planter to see if I could discover where the shots had come from. I own a gun but I hadn't even thought about taking it to a strip club.

I got to the end of the planter just in time to see a large black car speed through the synchronized green stop lights that make

Second Avenue, the best way to get across town. Unfortunately, it was too far away to get a license number. I turned back around just in time to see Kate run around the corner and up Pine Street.

. . .

CHAPTER TWO

The homicide detectives were a large black man in a cheap rumpled blue suit named Bill Brownwen, and his partner, a slender Asian woman named Tina Lo, fetchingly turned out in a black nylon jump suit that showed off her tight pert figure.

I don't get along too well with policemen. That probably doesn't surprise anyone reading this. And when this pair came in and the beat cop pointed me out, sitting at the bar with another 40-ounce PBR in front of me, I could tell by the frowns that this time was not going to be an exception to the rule.

I turned out to be right. My ponytail and half-assed investigator status, kind of on the edge of the legal boundaries, did not give them a feeling of good-guy bonding with me. My deeply ingrained wise-ass attitude toward people in any kind of authority, going all the way back to my split with the Marine Corps, when I was 22 years old and still just a dewy-eyed young killer, sort of sealed the deal.

Brownwen started the conversation. "Mr. Vieira, I hope watching a man die three feet in front of your face hasn't interfered with your beer drinking."

"Oh, not at all Detective, I've seen many men die in far less comfortable circumstances and managed to eat a full meal afterward. Goes with the good old government training."

From the way his head kept turning to peruse the bar and the bottles behind it, I got a feeling that Brownwen could have used a drink himself.

Tina Lo took over. "Did you know the victim?" She stared me straight in the eyes as either an unsuccessful attempt to intimidate me—look into my soul to detect lies—or as a signal that she had the hots for me. Somehow I did not think the latter one was the winner.

"Never saw him before tonight. I don't come here that often and after tonight I have a feeling I won't be back for a while."

"Why is that?"

"If I wanted to get shot at, I would have stayed in the Marines, or gotten a job like yours."

She raised an eyebrow and smirked as if I could not possibly handle her job.

She was right, of course. I couldn't tolerate the bullshit.

"Why were you here tonight?"

"Entertainment in the neighborhood."

She waited to hear what I considered entertainment.

"Amateur night at the Déjà Vu," I explained.

Her face went expressionless. "You like watching women get degraded and exploited?"

"Well, I like watching women dance around naked. As to who is getting exploited, I'm the one spending the money—on them. And one of them left with a couple of hundred bucks for about ten minutes of work. I didn't see anyone get degraded, but that might depend on your grade."

I wasn't making many points with this lady. Brownwen gave her a mental nudge with a raised eyebrow, and she backed off a little to give him a shot.

Maybe they were playing "big cop, little cop."

"Why was the bouncer standing right behind your table if you didn't know him?"

"There was a lady sitting with me. He might have known her, I don't know. And it's a pretty small patio."

"Who was the woman?"

"I didn't get her name. She bummed a cigarette and then dropped it. She bent over to pick it up and bullets started whizzing by my ear. I hit the deck with the lady's head between my legs. I got up a few seconds later just in time to see a big black sedan speeding off down the street and that's just about all I know."

"Just about?"

So the cops and I had a spirited semi-adversarial conversation until about three in the morning.

I ended up assuring them that I did not like people shooting at me, or the bouncer, or the window, or whoever they were shooting at. And if I thought of anything that would help, I would sure as hell let them know.

I finally retrieved my car from the market, cracked a PBR from the cooler I always keep under the dash (did I mention I'm just a bundle of bad habits?) and headed up Alaskan Way through the tunnel and out Aurora to my favorite sleazy motel, the Orion.

There are several reasons I choose to stay at the Orion. They give me a break on the price because my aversion to crack is such a refreshing aberration among their clientele. The managers, a Korean man, his American wife and their three very cute little kids, are fearless, take very little bullshit, and keep my car safe from depredations. Then there's the name "Orion" itself. A constellation I have gazed up at from many different seas around the world. It was also my dead hero uncle's middle name.

I didn't say all the reasons made good sense.

The sheets were clean and I hit them hard until around noon. Then I showered and started thinking about what to do with the rest of the day.

I had some money in the bank, but not a great comfort zone, so it was probably a good time for me to hunt up some more work.

Investigation work generally comes from lawyers, and since I'm not quite a licensed PI, mine comes from word of mouth and a solid reputation for being able to get usable material that their "legitimate" investigators would find helpful.

Not something you can cold canvas for door to door, so I headed for my office and principal schmoozing ground for talking to lawyers: the Central Saloon. Seattle's oldest second-class saloon, est. 1892, where my great friend, the lovely bartender Monica, already had a couple of PBRs shoved deeply into the ice, in the all-but-psychic knowledge that I would soon require them.

"Hi, Angus," she said with that 100-watt smile she was famous for. "First your medicine, then your messages."

She can always make me smile. "Please do me."

She slid a long-neck in front of me.

"So I have some messages?"

"Nope, but I didn't want to tell you that 'til you had a beer in front of you." She laughed and headed down the bar to take care of some other reprobate.

The Central is a Seattle landmark to me for much better reasons than its venerable age. It's a long fairly narrow room with a kitchen on one side and a long bar on the other leading to a stage at the back, where I have read poetry on many occasions. Next to the stage is a back door leading to the odiferous alley that runs behind 1st Avenue. Next to that door was part of my fifteen minutes of fame.

Three photos of me on stage in costumes that are mostly a black thong shaped like an elephant, I won't belabor where the trunk comes in, and boots and a strip of nylon tape diagonally across my chest that says "The Central." There was also a poem I wrote about this saloon.

These photos and my fame came about due to the slightly warped sense of humor of one of the owners of this dive, Jomo by name. Another friend who is well aware of the fact that I was born without the modesty gene.

In those dear dead days, Pioneer Square threw a pretty fair party each year for Mardi Gras with dancing and bead flinging, booby flashing and silly contests, like the "Mr. No Fat" and "Ms. No Fat" contests.

Jomo talked me into being the Central's contestant three years in a row. I gave it up the year I got badly beaten by a full-fledged drag queen another bar had called in as a ringer. Ahh, women judges.

I told Jomo, "God damn it, I don't enter their contests." Shortly thereafter, our new humorless and timid mayor cancelled Fat Tuesday anyway. My starring nylon 'crotch-elephant' and maniacal grin remain on the wall back where they won't scare the children.

I have, on occasion, been seen walking tourist girls back there in hopes of impressing them right out of their pants. This just about never works, but it was one more piece of proof that I have no shame, if proof was needed.

I know just about everyone who works or hangs regularly at this bar. So between Monica's wit and humor, and friends who actually have jobs coming in after work, several hours slipped by, and I caught enough of a buzz to realize I should head on up the road if I didn't want to leave my car there for the night.

Now usually I park right in front of the saloon but this night the Mariners were playing down at Safeco Field, and doing pretty well this year, so for once I had to park in an actual parking lot over on Occidental Avenue. I walked up Washington Street past an alley.

That's where the night suddenly went sideways. I've traipsed down a lot of dark streets in a lot of strange countries. I am fairly hard to sneak up on, but it can be done and right then somebody did it. A large hand vised my neck and whipped me into the alley.

I ran stumbling three or four yards, and was just turning around when a boot slammed me in the small of the back.

Big pain as I shot forward another six feet. This was getting very tedious quickly. I stuck up my right arm and went into a forward roll as a leg came out to trip me from the left.

So there were at least two of them.

I landed on my feet and whipped my right foot up in a spinning kick that connected with someone who gave a small grunt and pulled back a little, just as the big one landed a roundhouse to the left side of my head.

The night shifted to red for a minute and I was bent over a garbage can with my right arm jammed up between my shoulder blades. This guy was fast and strong, and way too good to be a street mugger—unless he had a real self-esteem issue.

So far there had been no conversation and I had not gotten even a glimpse at these assholes. I was pretty well pinned unless I wanted a badly broken arm, and that's the one I wipe my ass with, so I'm kind of fond of it.

I said, "Okay, dickhead, what do you want? I ain't got much money on me but I'll trade it for my arm."

It was the smaller one who answered in a voice lowered and altered until I couldn't really tell if its owner was a man or woman.

"Fuck your money," it said. "Where's the bitch? The one you were with last night at the bar?"

That one surprised me. "The dancer? How the fuck would I know! I don't even know her last name."

That seemed to give them pause. I sensed a silent dialogue between the two and then my arm was whipped even higher, and I was thrown further down the alley, belly flopping in a puddle I vainly hoped was not urine.

I got up slowly, taking some time to work my arm around. They were out of the alley and gone by the time I got to my feet. I hadn't gotten a clear look at them.

I made my way slowly to my car, working my arm. I stank of week-old piss, had blown out both the knees of my jeans, and my right arm was asking me for Ibuprofen and rum. It wasn't exactly a magic evening. It was time to head to the motel.

I had a nasty feeling that this wasn't the last time I'd have something to do with this pretty dancer.

. . .

CHAPTER THREE

At eleven the next morning, I was lying on the bed, lazily watching the Middle East beat itself to multiple deaths on CNN, when Monica called my cell phone.

"Hey, Angus, I hear through the Pioneer Square grapevine you left here and went out to vandalize our poor local alleys again."

"Well, you know me, anytime I see a puddle of week-old piss, I get the urge to mop it up with my face."

She had a great laugh. "So come on down to the Central and let me buy you lunch. Furious George made his famous meatloaf and I might have someone who wants to hire you, if you can tear yourself away from the alley floor."

My stomach growled with anticipation. "Mon, me deario, you have a wonderful talent for calling me when I'm naked. I find that I am completely happy with that, but you would probably find it a little disturbing. Let me find some non-bloodstained Levis and a clean strip-club T shirt, and I'm on my way. Stick some of that meatloaf aside, will ya?"

Half an hour later, I had shat, showered and shaved, crawled into a pair of well-worn black denims, and a Mary's Club (Portland's first topless establishment) T-shirt. The bathroom mirror reminded that my fashion sense stopped maturing at about mid-adolescence; some other parts of my personality did, too, as a matter of fact. But I was out the door before I gave a shit.

I got to the Central around 1 PM.

Monica saw me come in. She winked and slapped a PBR down in front of me, nodding to George in the kitchen.

"I have a big glass of house Merlot in the cooler for you when the food gets up. It won't take long to set you up. Meat loaf slathered in Central BBQ sauce with garlic mashed potatoes, on me, for defending the Square with your face."

She put her hand under my jaw and turned it both ways. "You've got some bruising but you can't really hurt a Scandinavian by hitting him in the head, so you'll live."

"I'm glad you think so, nurse, but will I be able to play the piano?"

"Not so I'd want to listen to it. You should maybe stick to the skin flute. After you eat, I'll tell you who came looking for you this morning."

George the cook sidled over while I ate, to make sure the food was up to his standards. It was hearty and garlicky, and with the chilled red (I know, I know, I'm a barbarian), I felt ready to fuck, fight, or foot race.

Monica came back to lean on the bar in front of me with a smile, a beer, and an embossed card. "Either you are gonna jump at this one or I'll have to re-evaluate everything I know about your horn-dog personality."

She slid the card in front of me.

The card read, "Walter Hickok, Real Estate Properties Entrepreneur."

"I know that name from somewhere."

"You sure should," she said. "He owns a lot of the local strip clubs, where you've left DNA evidence from your saliva, or something else, on the couches. He also owns a lot of bars where the girls wear at least their bras and panties and a butt-wad of other stuff. He's a very rich man, and he wants to hire you for some reason, and here's the kicker: He sent a beautiful blonde, in a tiny little skirt that just barely covered her trigger, down here to find you. She didn't know your name, but from her description, it didn't take too much of a detective to figure out who she was talking about. I said I would see if I could find you and she said that you could come up to Mr. Hickok's office anytime between then, which was right when I opened, 'til 8 o'clock tonight. You see the address? Two blocks from here in a corner office in the Pioneer Square Building, second floor overlooking the Pergola."

The Pioneer Square Building is one of my favorites. If I ever actually made enough money to require a real office with a real secretary, like Mike Hammer, I couldn't think of a better place to hang my fedora. Note to self: Look for a low-priced but way cool fedora.

Hickok's office was up a wide, real-wood stairway in one corner of the second floor. The door was open and I walked into his office.

I saw what Monica meant about a real short skirt.

Facing me—well that's not quite the right word—In front of me, a woman was bent over rummaging around in the lowest drawer of a filing cabinet. She was wearing a very bright red pair of very tight panties over her heart-shaped butt. Above this was a very ineffective strip of black fabric, which might have been meant to represent a skirt.

I just stopped to admire the view until she straightened up, turned around, and gave me a tight-lipped smile, to let me know she knew just what I was looking at.

"Is there some other way I can help you? Or did you just come to admire the view?"

I gave her my most lecherous smile. As you might imagine, I'm fairly good at that.

"That is always a dangerous question to ask the likes of me, but we can get back to that later. For now the question might be, how do you, or is it Mr. Hickok, think that I can be of help?"

"Ah," she studied a piece of paper on her desk. "You would be Mr. Angus Vieira?"

"Angus will do."

"Walter is in there waiting for you. You can go right on in." She gave me a small mischievous smile that made me think she was still thinking about me perusing her scarlet butt.

In a minute I got a little different idea.

Sitting behind a large old desk of real wood, staring down at the statue of Chief Sealth raising his arm to the bewildered flock of tourists milling around, waiting to be led to underground Seattle, was a fairly short man with a salt and pepper beard, grey hair and cold eyes that looked like they'd been around the block even more often than I had.

Walter Hickok turned and stared at me like he couldn't quite figure out if he wanted to throw me a biscuit or pick up a rock and shoo me out of his yard.

"Where the fuck is my daughter?" he said in a very quiet voice that stirred the short hairs on the back of my neck.

"Who the fuck is your daughter, and how the fuck should I know?" This wasn't starting out too well, but he irritated me first.

We stared at each other for a while, and I was just about ready to turn around and wave goodbye to Ms. Tight Panties when he blinked first. "Okay, I may be wound a little too tight today. Let's start over, shall we? Please sit down, Mr. Vieira."

"We shall, and thank you I will." I sat across the desk from him as he almost visibly got his angry self under control.

"My daughter is Kate Hickok. Do you know her, by any chance? She seems to have gone missing. I went to her apartment to look for her and your card was in the middle of her floor."

He pointed at my card, which I now noticed lying in the middle of his desk. We trained investigators don't miss a thing. Eventually.

"I think I met your daughter a couple of days ago. The girl I met was named Kate, and I gave her my card. She about 5' 10" slender but nicely girlish?" I was trying to keep it circumspect for old dad.

"Sounds like her, short brown hair and a great rack."

So much for circumspection.

I thought I could talk straight to this man. He appeared to be genuinely worried about his daughter and I had a feeling she might have her tail in a tight enough crack to need some worrying about.

I started at the Athenian meeting and went right on through the strip contest, without really emphasizing what a nice ass the lady had, and the shooting at the bar. Lastly I told him about the melee in the alley and the questions the tag team asked me.

He just sat there with a small frown for a few minutes after I finished. And I just watched him, giving him time to digest it all. I would have bet the farm that all of this was news to him.

I finally decided I'd given him enough time to think about it. "She's a big girl. What makes you think she's in trouble?"

He went on thinking about it for a minute.

I got the definite impression he didn't like answering anyone's questions.

He started off slowly, but gathered speed as he went along.

"Kate and I have had our share of troubles. I don't know if you are a father of girls, but they have their own unique set of problems growing up."

I decided not to tell him I had more experience being one of the father's problems.

He continued, "But once a week, we get together for a brunch or dinner—always the same day. That was yesterday. If one or the other of us is busy, we always call each other. Celeste is always here to answer the phone and she didn't get a call. Neither did my cell phone and I got worried."

He shot me a concerned-father look. I tried to look sympathetic.

"When I hadn't heard from her by late last night, I went knocking on her door. She didn't answer. So I went in."

He paused here, to look me in the eye, like he needed to clarify this.

"I have a key, because I'm her father and her landlord. She has an apartment down on First Avenue, not far from that bar you hang out at."

I nodded because he paused again and I didn't really know what else to do.

"The place looked like she had packed in a big hurry—clothes all over the floor. Her suitcase and some of her toiletries were gone—probably a backpack, too."

He turned to stare out the window. "I am not universally loved in this town. I have some enemies. I don't think she was kidnapped, because anyone who was packing for her wouldn't have made such a mess."

He turned back to me. "I know my daughter and I think she was scared by something. But I can't figure out why she didn't call me. When I found your card, your name rang a small bell, so I called some of the lawyers I know in the area. As you can imagine, I do some business with a lot of them. They told me you were pretty competent and straight.

But I decided to send Celeste down to the Central to ask you to come up here instead of calling you."

I had wondered about that.

He spread his hands and shrugged. "That's about all I know. I need someone to look into this and find her. Or find out what happened to her, and you seem like the best choice. As far as I know, you aren't my enemy, or in the pay of someone who doesn't like me. You do this for a living and are considered pretty good at it. I have the money to finance you. Will you take the job?"

He took an envelope out of his pocket and put it on the desk. It was a pretty thick envelope.

"There is five thousand dollars in this envelope, and more if you find her or need it. It's in cash because I don't like paper trails. You don't have to give me written reports, but you do have to keep me informed. What do you think?"

It wasn't just the fact that I was looking at more money than I'd seen since I stopped being a merchant marine, but that did help. I already had a gut feeling that this lady might be in need of some help, and I was a lot better than nothing.

I nodded and picked up the envelope. "Give me the key to her place. That's where I'll start looking. I need some kind of clue or it's a mighty big world."

It was a pretty spring day in Seattle. Upper 60s, light overcast. Pioneer Square was one of my favorite spots in the whole world. I kind of sauntered south down First Avenue, giving a wave to Monica as I passed the Central, to a building only a few doors south—a narrow brick four-story recently refurbished. This was a spendy place to live.

One of the keys Hickok gave me opened the front door. Inside the small vestibule was a list of the tenants. All just last names except for "Allure Models" on the second floor. A Hickok was marked as 3A.

I started up the stairs as a willowy young woman with shoulder-length blonde curls came down, wearing a skirt just a little longer than Hickok's secretary. I didn't get to see its color, or if she had underwear on at all, but it was a near thing. She gave me an appraising glance with a small smirk.

Well, she could be a model.

The second floor hallway was short and ended with one very sturdy-looking door, with a full length mirror next to it. A small name plate next to the door just said "Allure."

There was a bell next to the door, with a little light above it.

I knew that I had five grand in my pocket, but somehow, I didn't think that would last too long on the other side of this door.

I continued up to the third floor where there were two doors at opposite ends of the hallway.

The one closest to First Avenue was marked A and the key fit, letting me into a long narrow apartment, the kind that calls itself a loft, here in the artsy-fartsy Square.

Light-yellow main room walls were framed with posters advertising various local rock bands, playing at places like the Crocodile, the old Larry's Greenfront (I still miss that place) and even the Central. It was strange that I'd never run into this young lady right around here.

Full ashtrays, comfortable leather futon couch, desk in the corner with an Apple Computer. I might have to look into that later, but given my limited skills in that area, I might bring someone back to help me with that.

I continued down the hall to the kitchen. Neat and functional, pans hanging from a rack on the wall and the knife rack looked professional grade.

The bathroom was a different story. Cosmetics. Lotions, lipsticks, perfumes and tampons were scattered all over the floor. Someone had either been in a big hurry to find something, or, more likely, I'd say, was picking through several years of the detritus that accumulates in a girl's search for eternal youth and beauty and the sweetest of smells.

I tiptoed through this stuff to pee in the toilet. Yes, I had to lift the seat and I did it with a handkerchief, the same one I used to put it back down again and flush. So far, I hadn't left any fingerprints. It might not be important but there was no reason not to be a little careful.

If the bathroom was a mess, the bedroom was a disaster area. It looked like a level four tornado spent some quality time in the women's apparel department of one of the 'spendier' department stores, maybe bringing along some stuff it picked up at Victoria's Secret.

Queen-sized bed with purple silk sheets all mussed up. Let's see, where had I run into purple sheets lately?

There was a framed photo face down in the middle of the bed that I once again used the handkerchief to flip over.

A naked lady covering her crotch with one hand, her finger in her mouth, and a wide-eyed look of mock shocked innocence on her face looked out at me—and in the lower corner, a handwritten message, "Love the good licks," followed by hearts, Xs and Os, and the letter A.

I knew the hand that covered her crotch was covering a little curly brown Hitler's mustache.

Hello, Amanda.

I might not be Arsène Lupin, that fictional gentleman thief the French dig so much, but I thought I knew where to look next.

■ ■ ■

CHAPTER FOUR

I knew that Amanda usually worked at night so I was pretty sure I could still catch her at her apartment house. That seemed like a good idea because I thought I was going to want this conversation to be nice and private. Well, maybe not nice, but certainly private.

Amanda's far from a shy girl, but there might be some things even she would want to keep from her work girlfriends.

I took a nice spring afternoon walk down Broadway, watching the garishly dressed people who stroll here at any time of the day or night, in all their notorious glory.

Then I cut over a block and headed up the walk to Ms. Smith's apartment. The front door was propped open. That interested me a little.

I walked up the carpeted stairs to Amanda's third-floor apartment. There, too, the door was propped ajar.

Amanda was obviously expecting someone. Not me because I didn't call to tell her I was coming. Ah well, the girl loves surprises so I walked in through the entry hallway and into her apartment.

She had a sunny living room with a black leather sofa, a recliner and a huge flat-panel TV. I could get comfortable here. I certainly was comfortable in the bedroom.

Jackie Rome, one of my favorite local singer songwriters and a very sexy lady, was gushing out of the elaborate CD speaker system.

The sliding door to Stormy's small veranda was open and the girl herself was lying on a chaise lounge on her back, naked of course. Tough to keep this lady in her clothes, but then again who would want to.

She was watching me with a small smile on her face and the dreamy eyes of the recently stoned.

I wandered out there, perched next to her with a hand on her nice sweaty knee.

Her little Hitler mustache was gone. Her crotch was as hairless now as it was when she slid out of her momma's crotch.

"You lost your little nose tickler, baby."

She threw her other leg way out to the side to give me a better view of her nether lips, giving herself a little rub.

"Hi there, my big old stud muffin, you didn't get it good enough last time?" She gave herself another little rub and her lips started to pooch out a little.

I reminded myself that I was here on another kind of business.

"This is a whole different day, sweetheart, and unfortunately your sweet-hole is a whole different subject this afternoon. I came to see if you could help me find a friend of yours whose daddy is worried about her."

She closed her legs and gave me a slight frown.

Oh well, maybe I could cheer her up later.

"Rub some suntan lotion on my back," she said, flipping over on her stomach.

"Gladly." I grabbed the lotion bottle.

"How do you know Kate's daddy?"

"I didn't until today. He found my card on the floor of her apartment when he went to look for her because she didn't show up for their weekly brunch date. He thinks she took off for parts unknown in a big hurry. So do I."

She gave her head a shake and wriggled as I squirted white goo from a tube onto her back.

"I don't really like Daddy Hickok nearly as much as I like his daughter. And I don't really trust him at all," she said.

"I can't say I trust him much, but I have pretty good instincts for telling when someone is lying, and I do really believe he's worried about her."

"Well, Walter Hickok might be the one to fool you; I could tell you a whole bunch of stories about him. Kate and I talked about him, a lot."

"I found your picture on her bed upside down. And my card, that supposedly fell out of her pocket was on the floor, Walter said. Could be she wanted to get me to come and talk to you, if I wasn't too dim to figure it out."

I was rubbing my way down her back with the fragrant lotion and was now at her firmly round buttocks.

"Hmmmm, that feels pretty good. So if Daddy Hickok hired you does that mean he gave you a bunch of money to run around finding our Kate?"

I chuckled and squirted some white lotion in her butt crack.

"Yup, if you tell me what I want to hear, I could swing a couple of hundred at your pretty ass."

Her legs parted a few inches as I ran my finger down her cleft to her little winker and slid the tip of my finger in.

"Unh, don't they say that's where the sun don't shine?"

"No sense taking any chances."

She wiggled a little. "You're probably right about that. If you make it three hundred, I'll tell you what you want to hear and let you do what you obviously want to do."

I slid my finger in a little further. "That sounds like a very good deal." Her butt went a little further in the air. "I aim to please."

"Kate and I are friends. Sometimes we fool around a little if we're both feeling horny and a little stoned. We're both a little bi, and her pussy is mighty tasty. So after that bouncer got whacked when she bent over, she was totally freaked out. She was shitting bricks by the time she got here at four in the morning and woke me up. She doesn't know who is doing it, or why, but some weird shit had been happening to her lately. She thinks she's being followed, people maybe getting into her apartment. Something is going down. She doesn't trust her daddy either, although she couldn't think of a reason why he would want to hurt her. They get along pretty well. That's why she entered the Vu contest. Build up a little get-out-of-town fund, just in case. I calmed her down some, got her a little stoned and said I'd help as much as I could. She is a girlfriend, and I don't have a bunch of them. Some of the girls in this business can be pretty bitchy and kinda cutthroat. So I have this kinda boyfriend, a fisherman who goes crabbing in Alaska. He's out on the boat now, probably will be for another month or so. Well, this apartment comes with a parking spot in a lot down the block and I don't drive anymore after a little DUI problem I got into a couple of years ago with the cops and shit. Anyway, he left his car there and gave me the keys because he trusts me and said he wants to marry me and settle down when he stops being a crazy fisherman." Her brow knits into a little frown for an instant, "And, stops blowing so much money up his nose.

"So I loaned her the car and four hundred dollars, called it my good deed for the day. Uh, do that real slow. I don't do this with very many people but you seem to know what you're doing and I do like it, just do it gently."

With my finger still deep in her ass, I moved around until my lap was in her face. She undid my belt and rubbed her face on my Levi's. My cock was stiffening in happy anticipation. That kinky devil did have a mind of its own.

"What kind of car? Let's get that out of the way so I can give you the buggering you so richly deserve."

"Ooooh buggering, oh goody. I don't hear that word very often. My purse is on the coffee table, if you will please hand it to me. You probably should take your finger out of my ass first, though."

I brought her a big leather purse, like a small overnight bag.

I could take a hint. I got three one hundred dollar bills out and laid them on top of her hand.

"That's my nice dirty pervert. Why don't you get nice and naked while I find the information?" She rummaged while I stripped.

"Here it is. A nice car, too. A 1966 Impala convertible with bucket seats, black inside and out. I hope she takes care of it. The license plate says FISHUN. That Tommy loves his car. He likes me to blow him while we drive down I-5. Says he doesn't know if he is coming or going. When you find her, make sure she brings it back to me."

Amanda handed me a slip of paper with that information on it. "And looky what else I found." She waved a shiny silver vibrator under my nose as she giggled. "She headed south. Says she's always kind of wanted to be a stripper but didn't want to do it in the same town where her daddy lives. I gave her the name of the manager of Union Jack's in Portland. Big Jim Dunn. He's a big ol' sweetheart. That's about all I know 'til she calls me. It's only been a couple of days but if she does I will tell her you are looking for her. Now, you've got to promise to be a little slow and gentle, you little Butthole Surfer."

She got on her hands and knees with her ass pushed out over the back end of the chaise lounge and her dildo sliding in and out of her slippery lips.

I moved behind her rubbing a lot of suntan lotion on my lizard.

Johnny Wadd, the porn legend, is supposed to have said that there is no difference between a woman's pussy and a man's ass hole. Well, I have never fucked a man's asshole, but a woman's asshole was probably similar and it always seems very different from a pussy or a mouth to me. I love them all.

That poor bastard Wadd had a huge dick, but maybe it didn't have many nerve endings. Amanda yipped and grunted as I slowly slid up her poop chute. I could feel the vibrations from her toy as it moved in and out of her pussy. I tried to take it slowly but that didn't last too long.

None of Amanda's neighbors could look directly onto her balcony, but I wondered if anyone down on the street or in another apartment was listening with voyeuristic amusement at the moans and grunts.

Ms. Smith was very enthusiastic and we even came at about the same time. She beat me by a little and that's the best way.

Afterward she flopped on her stomach and mumbled about taking a little nap.

I used her shower to wash my butt burglar and got dressed slowly, with an unstoppable smile.

I headed out her front door, which I remembered I had left ajar.

It would have been very amusing if whomever she was expecting had come in while we were thrashing around like frogs in a puddle.

Just as I touched the doorknob, a small noise behind me made me turn. Maybe I was going to get one last hug.

Not quite. Something very hard crashed into the back of my head and time went away for a while.

■ ■ ■

Pain pulled me back to consciousness and the large impassive face of Sgt. Brownwen, staring down at me like he wondered how I got stuck to the bottom of his shoe.

I put a hand on the back of my head very gently. Yup, it was bloody. My right knee was aching, too, and I noticed I was at the bottom of the flight of stairs leading to Amanda's apartment.

"Sgt. Brownwen, did you happen to see somebody with a baseball bat with my blood on it run past as you came in?"

"Cut the crap, Vieira. How is it every time I come across you, you just happen to be in the vicinity of somebody's violent death?"

"Hey, I'm feeling kinda run over right now, but I'm a long way from dead."

He was very quiet for several moments. Just staring down at me until even I started to get nervous. "What don't I know about here?"

He stuck a big hand under my arm and, almost gently, raised me to my feet, steadying me as I wobbled.

Lo, his partner, moved up on the other side, tiny in comparison but surprisingly strong when she took my other arm.

"Come outside with me for a minute. Got something I want to show you," Brownwen growled.

We moved slowly down the stairs.

There were a bunch of people, men and women, some in police uniform, standing around on the planting strip in front of the building. They slowly parted as we approached.

Amanda was lying on the grass, staring sightlessly at the blue sky. Still very naked, now very dead.

I felt like I wanted to puke.

For one insane moment I was afraid I would break into hysterical giggles, then my legs wobbled a little and the two cops tightened their grip.

Everyone was very quiet for a minute and then Brownwen spoke.

"I wonder if, when we autopsy this poor little stripper, will we find any of your semen up her snatch?"

I shook my head slowly, knowing that what I was going to say next was going to

make for a very long day.   But they were
going to find out anyway.

"No, but you probably will up her ass."

I felt like I was standing in front of a very
large fan, and someone had just thrown a big
bucket of shit at it.

■ ■ ■

CHAPTER FIVE

Brownwen and Lo helped me into the back seat of a plain black Crown Victoria and got in the front. Both turned to look at me with identical quizzical frowns on their very different faces.

They probably were a very effective team.

This time Tina Lo started it. "That's a big old bump you have on the back of your head, Mr. Vieira. Do you want us to take you to Harborview, or shall we go straight to jail?"

I did have a large round knob on the back of my head, kind of like someone glued half of a billiard ball to the back of my head with my blood.

"Hmmm, let's see, Harborview will take all day to get me some aspirin and not much sympathy, jail will take me all day to get a baloney sandwich and no sympathy at all. So if it's okay with you two, let's see if we can find me a different destination altogether. I don't know who killed Amanda Smith, but I know who didn't. That would be me. She and I are, were, pretty good fuck buddies and I stopped by this afternoon to see if she was in the mood for some consensual sex."

"Anal sex." Brownwen had a small smirk as he glanced at his partner.

"Some girls like a little fudge packing on occasion, keeps then regular."

Tina Lo looked at me like she had just swallowed a worm that looked a lot like me.

On the other hand that sounded callous even to me.

So I took a deep breath and blew it at the cops. "Look, I liked her. I wasn't in love with her but she was a ballsy girl with a good sense of humor, and we had fun. I do not know who killed her but I promise you that if somehow I find out, I'll let you know ASAP. The same killer smashed me on the back of the head and threw me down the stairs, remember? I don't think you think I did that to myself just so I could hang around 'til you showed up so we could have this conversation."

They peered back at me, like they were expecting more.

"I won't get in the way of your investigation but if I find out anything or think of anything that can help in any way, I'll sure get it to you. My car is down by Dick's. How about you drop me off there?"

Yeah, right, I knew that was going to happen.

The disparate duo stared at each other solemnly for several moments exchanging psychic information.

Brownwen got out and opened the back door for me. "The walk will do you good."

I don't know if the walk did me any good. Each step sent little wriggly pains shooting around my skull, but at the end of it there was a Dick's Deluxe Burger.

This was the second time I'd been here in a very few days and some people might consider that a bit unhealthy but the frequency at which I was getting beat up these same few days made me wonder if I had to worry too much about long range health issues.

I almost took one of the all-beef patties and rubbed it on the back of my head, but that probably wouldn't have helped much, and it might have gotten me some odd looks even on Broadway.

Rooby started with her trademark rumble and I headed back to the Orion Motel to gather my travel pack. That didn't take too long and an hour later I was doing seventy miles an hour headed north on I-5 toward my "summer estate."

That's what I call the many acres of gently-sloping, well-manicured lawns, a hot tub, showers, toilets, and a big tent for barbeques... and sometimes karaoke. It is a nudist camp on the outskirts of Mount Vernon, with a reasonably-priced and friendly pub just a few miles away.

My palatial home there is a twelve foot trailer, close to the toilets and parked in the shade of a large pine tree. It's really very comfortable, as long as it was just me, or me and a very close friend. Two or more friends better bring a tent or rent the comfortable cabin next door.

I like running around naked, and I like nudists. It seems to me that people who have gotten over the social dogma that "thou shalt not show thy genitalia to anyone but thine current significant other" have usually become interesting people in a number of areas.

The afternoon traffic through Everett was slow and cumbersome but it broke loose around the Indian Casinos and the rest of the journey was swift and pleasant.

I arrived at the camp around dusk. I washed four ibuprofen down with a can of PBR, packed a different travel pack for an extended journey and read a few pages of Don Marquis's *Life and Times of Archy and Mehitabel*. I don't know why but he soothes and amuses me when I've had a tough day, and I'd had a couple of them.

I slept like the dead for about nine hours.

The next morning I tossed my travel pack in Rooby's voluminous trunk, along with a cooler full of PBR and ice, and turned down the trailer's heater. I was set for a trip that could last as long as it had to, or considering the lethal nature of whoever seemed to be after Kate, maybe forever as far as I was concerned.

Amanda sprawling naked and dead on her own front lawn kept dancing to the front of my brain.

My dentist scolds me for grinding my teeth while I sleep. Well, this was a wide-awake tooth grinding morning. I wanted this guy or guys and it would be real nice to save Kate's ass in the bargain.

That thought brought a quick flash of Kate's ass on stage dancing around. I shook that one off for now and locked the trailer and started the five-mile drive back to I-5.

I thought about what I had to go on and it wasn't a lot. Daddy Hickok did not seem to be the culprit, by my reasoning, but I remembered what Amanda said, and he might be fooling me. If he was trying to make her dead, he might be sending me after her as a bird dog, me doing the pointing and him just sauntering up with the shotgun, but that just didn't make much sense to me.

He could have just thrown her off the bridge at Deception Pass, or poisoned her brunch croissant, or on and on. And he had also fronted me five grand to go looking for her when he had a lot of guys already on salary, and while he was a very rich man, from what I hear, I did not get the impression he was real open-handed with a buck.

I did know what kind of car Kate was driving and possibly her first contact. So I pointed Rooby's nose south, jacked her up to 75, cracked a beer, with an eye out for the cops, and got comfortable for the two-hundred mile drive to Portland, Oregon.

Rooby, of course, would not go two hundred miles without getting very thirsty. We have a lot in common: thirsty most of the time, with a lot of miles under our wheels, but we get the job done.

A couple of gas stations and piss stops later, I got off the freeway in downtown Portland, a city with a lot more frustrating one way streets than Seattle would ever brag about.

After circling a few blocks I headed east on Burnside, over the freeway and up the street a few blocks to my favorite motel. It's my favorite not so much because it's all that different from a lot of other medium-priced motels along Burnside and out Sandy

Boulevard, but because it was directly across the street from Union Jack's Nude Dancing Emporium.

Union Jack's is one of my favorite places in America to watch naked women dance for several reasons. Long-neck PBRs are cheap and plentiful. You can drink one while you smoke a cigarette and a beautiful lady bends over and shakes her ass directly in your face for a tip of a couple of bucks.

To paraphrase an old country song, "If heaven ain't a lot like Union Jack's, I don't wanna go."

I stowed my gear in Room 22 and headed across the street to get all of the things I just mentioned, and a map of the strip joints in Portland – plus a talk with Jim Dunn, the manager that Amanda had mentioned. He was my best hope on this faint and tenuous trail I was following.

I have known Big Jim for a long time. As a matter of fact we were both Seafarer's International Union members before we each "swallowed the anchor," meaning gave up the seagoing life. Me, to do whatever the hell it was I was doing, and him, to run various bars in Seattle and titty bars in Portland. He must be a lot smarter than I am.

I walked into the dark smoky bar and didn't have to look too far to find Jim. He was sitting back in the corner by the main stage with a frosted mug of beer and a stack of one-dollar bills in front of him.

I bought a long-neck from the pretty redheaded bartender and sat down next to him.

"Yo, my union brother, help me evaluate the fresh meat."

He stuck a couple of ones on the tip rail in front of me.

"After these ya gotta deal your own."

"Thanks, big brother, I'll be happy to."

A lithe little blonde girl, who might not yet be old enough to drink (in Portland you only have to be 18 to shuck your drawers on stage, you just can't drink there between shows—go figure), came crawling along the tip rail butt naked. She gave me a grin and leaned down to stick her head between Jim's thighs and shook it back and forth with her tight young rear end wiggling in front of my face. She was giggling, Jim was chuckling, and I laughed out loud—a jolly afternoon at the old Union Jack's.

After she collected her dollars from all over the stage, put on her panties, waved and grinned her way off stage, Jim turned to give me an appraising look.

"Looks like something's got its teeth in your tail."

Big Jim Dunn was a very large man with a very bushy medium length beard and looks like the guy who played Hayden on the television series *Northern Exposure*: tall, big, with a great gravelly voice. He is as straight an arrow as I ever met in all his dealings. The girls who worked for him mostly like him a lot, which isn't always the case with strip joint managers.

The DJ in the corner interrupted us to announce the next dancer. My ears pricked up as he said, "And next for your perverted viewing pleasure we give you Bridget coming all the way from Seattle to make your pants all bulgy so get your hands out of your laps and into your wallets, guys. And remember all these girls are available later for private dances."

A slender and leggy big-titted beauty, with a mane of platinum blonde hair that reached past her waist, came jumping on stage and started climbing the center pole.

When she got about ten feet up the pole she wrapped her legs around it and stuck there upside down as she pulled her G-string down...no, I guess up to her knees exposing her completely shaved and very kissable pussy. I happen to know how kissable it is because I have kissed it on many occasions.

"I know that girl very well," I said to Jim. "I'm glad to see her."

"Yah," he grunted," all these bitches are a little nuts. But I like her a lot now that she's kicked the crack pipe. I'm always glad to see her when she comes down from Seattle to take a breather. She isn't as young as some of the other girls but she's got a butt tight enough to crack walnuts and she knows how to work it. She makes good bucks."

I put a couple of bucks on the tip rail as she slid rapidly down the pole, stopping just short of smashing her head into the hardwood floor. She knew what she was doing.

She somersaulted my way just to show me how tight her butt really was and then grabbed the dollars and put them in my mouth and then took them out again with her large firm top-of-the-line breasts.

"Hello, my dirty, dirty man. Are you going to give me a dance later?"

I mumbled in the affirmative and nodded, with my face still buried between her tits.

"Oh, goody." She finally let me come up for air as she cavorted off waving her buttocks at me.

I looked back at Jim who was grinning at me.

"Yes, she's right about the dirty, dirty guy part. But right now I'm actually working. I'm looking for a girl who might be dancing here... or somewhere in Portland."

I pulled out the picture of Kate I had cut out of the *Exotic Underground* I found in her apartment and handed it to him. He just glanced at it and gave it back.

"That would be Salome. She is a pretty one. Real name is Kate Hickok but you already know that."

I nodded. "Is she in town?"

Jim shrugged. "I kinda doubt it, but she was last week. She danced here for a couple of days and made good money and then was just gone. I'll tell you who might know—your friend Bridget there. I think she was staying with her."

Now I had two reasons to talk to my fuck buddy Danielle, a/k/a Bridget. And only one of them was in my pants. So after she finished dancing on the big stage and the smaller one up front and took a bathroom break, I walked up to her at the bar and gave her a big hug and a butt pat.

"Hi, beautiful. Kinda far from Rick's, aren't you?"

"Hi, cutie." Her hand dropped to the front of my pants and gave me a quick rub. She put her mouth next to my ear and whispered breathily, "I am real horny, lover, and this place has cameras all over the private dancing spots. Don't buy dances here. Let me come over to your room. I'll be off work in about an hour."

"Room 22," I murmured back.

I drank one more beer, gave a few more girls some dollar bills, said goodbye to Jim and headed back across the street for a quick shower. I wanted my cock to be highly kissable.

Half an hour later I was squeaky clean and Jovan-Musky. I know that sounds a little "frou-frou," but a lot of women tell me they love how I smell, so I'll just frou-frou away, thank you.

I was wearing my lucky neon-red boxer shorts with the gape-open front, when Danielle knocked on the door and came rushing in.

"Hi, lover. Oooh, you smell good!"

See what I mean?

"Don't hug me right now. My last customer is a guy that spends a lot of money on me and we did some private dances and he came all over my ass."

As she was saying this, she was rushing around the small room shedding purse, practically an overnight bag of black leather, her top—no bra on those girls, shoes—tall and shiny, her little black skirt and a tiny red thong that really deserved the name "anal-floss."

"You can wash it for me." She headed for the shower with me literally hot on her tail.

I had some Kate-centered questions to ask this lady, but timing is everything, my hard-on reminded me.

Once she was clean and only a little damp I flopped on the bed on my back and she knew what that meant. As I said, this wasn't our first rodeo. She straddled my head with a knee by each ear and I buried my nose in her ass as I furiously licked her clitty. I could feel her lips thicken—she got very slippery, very soon. She started making ladylike grunting noise, as I put two fingers up her ass—very tight and very hot. She, of course, was grunting around my cock.

She was a world class cocksucker.

When she came, my beard was drenched, and for a minute, I thought I'd end up with a couple of broken fingers. A second later, she took my cock deep in her mouth and I came down her throat. It took a while for the room to stop vibrating but eventually I got around to asking Danielle some questions about Kate Hickok.

"She worked with me at UJ's for two days last week. We did a couple of doubles with some of the big spenders and I let her stay in the other bed in my motel, which by the way is the same as your motel. I'm up on the second floor." She winked.

"She has a future in this crazy business if she keeps at it. She's beautiful and she's losing her modesty at a pretty good rate. She was real scared about something though and kept saying she was still way too close to Seattle and whoever is after her. So I gave her the name of a friend of mine who does this in Reno. If I didn't trust you a lot, I wouldn't tell you her name, but I do think you want to help her. And she might need some help."

I just nodded and waited.

"I told her to go see Tess at Diamond Dolls, just off Fourth Street in Reno."

She started kissing my ear. "Mmmmmm, your beard smells like pussy. I like that."

"Well you have the softest lips I've ever come across," I chuckled. "Did you like the fingers in your ass?"

"You know I love that. It makes me come so hard. Did I ever tell you about the first time I ever got butt-fucked? It was back in the days when I had this boyfriend named David and we were both still smoking crack. He was Big D and I was Little D because my real name is Danielle, as you know. Well, one night I was supposed to go dance at a bachelor party and Big D was going to drive me, so he picked me up in a new—well, new to us—camper van he had just bought, and said, 'Fuck it, Lil' D, I don't want you working tonight.' He had a bag of rock and we headed down to park by Lake Washington and got really ripped."

Danielle was straddling my belly now as I lay back and enjoyed the story and the feel of her still wet crotch on me.

"Well, the last thing I remember is him saying, 'Oh baby, can I put it up your ass?' and then he shoved it in like uuunh." She shoved herself forward. "And then he came harder than any time I've ever made him come like uuunh uuunh uuunh." She was laughing and thrusting.

"So the next morning I wake up and my ass feels all wet and I think I've shit myself. I jump up on my knees and I'm gonna open the door and squat beside the camper. But I hear these construction guys across the street, talking real loud like, 'Ya, I can smell the crack from here.' So I couldn't do that and I started shaking Big D awake. I finally got the nerve to stick my hand back there and fortunately it was just come."

She waited until I stopped laughing to get off my chest.

She had her top and panties on in thirty seconds. No sense getting her panties all goopy.

I gave her three hundred bucks and rubbed my beard all over her face.

"Mmmmmmm, pussy," she said. "You are such a freak, I love it. Do you want to hear one more story? It isn't even sexy, it's just the nastiest story I know."

I just lay there and nodded.

"Well, this happened right after I got out of rehab; I was clean but jittery, trying to stay clean, so I was drinking massive amounts of water and coffee. It was in the morning and I drove to Wal-Mart, because I needed a couple of thing, I dunno, toilet paper, mouth wash and something else.

"Well, there I was, wearing my pajama bottoms and a little top—walking with my shopping cart and it felt like I had to fart. But it came out in a 'whoosh' like diarrhea. I felt this warm wet stuff running down my leg and I thought, 'Oh, shit'—which I was sure it was, of course.

"I turned in to the ladies' department and grabbed the first pair of pants my size I found, and headed back to the checkout counter. I thought of going to the bathroom but I decided 'What the fuck, I don't care, it's Wal-Mart."

"Of course, there's only one checker working, but there was only one lady in line ahead of me and it looks like she only had one thing in her cart. So I slip right in behind her. And then she started to pull all of these things out of her cart—she's got fifteen things up there.

"Then this really hot guy comes up and stands in line behind me. I'm thinking, 'Oh my God, was there a big stain back there and can you smell me? Do I stink?' This is taking forever and I don't dare turn around." She shook her head and laughed high and merry.

"So when I finally check out, I turn around to the counter and I back out of Wal-Mart. This is just such a nasty story; I have got to tell someone. So I tell some of the girl's at Rick's, where I was working. Pretty soon everyone knows it, and I get ragged about it a lot. I still do. Last week I text messaged a guy who was a bouncer there to see if he wanted to meet for lunch and he texted me back, 'Does Bridget shit in a Wal-Mart.'"

She jumped up and down shaking her head. "I work at Union J's at noon, you gonna come see me?" She was rubbing my Johnson, but it was still kind of sleepy.

"I'd love to, dear, but I gotta find Kate. I'll be on the road—maybe on my way back."

I was hoping there would be a way back.

. . .

CHAPTER SIX

I've never been fond of mornings. I've always felt that anything you can do in the morning, you could do as well or better in the afternoon, when everyone was in a better mood. But I was at least four days behind Kate and I still had a feeling that I was not the only one sniffing after that particular shapely tail. So I was packed and getting ready to check out by ten A.M.

A lot of morning people won't be very impressed by that. But since I usually get out around by the crack of noon, I was kind of proud of myself as I walked to the motel office.

My cell phone rang. It was Walter Hickok's office.

"Mr. Vieira? This is Celeste, of Mr. Hickok's office. You might remember me?"

"Please make that Angus, and yes, I seem to recall seeing you fundamentally. Tell me, what color panties are we wearing today?"

She gave a throaty chuckle. "Take a guess."

"How about red?"

Another chuckle. This girl would be a natural for phone sex. "Mr. Hickok would like to speak to you."

I heard her murmur something and then another phone picked up.

Walter Hickok's quietly menacing voice came through the line. "Hello, Angus. I think the understanding we have is that I am to be kept informed as you wander around spending my money."

I didn't think he was trying to be menacing particularly, it was just either a habit or a state of mind.

"So why haven't I heard from you in a while?"

That was because I still hadn't figured out what side of the equation to put him on, but I didn't think I should tell him that.

"You are right, that is the deal and maybe I should have called before this but, I've been wandering real hard and fast. A lot has been going on but I didn't have any hard information yet. I'm in Portland right now. Kate was here a few days ago and now she's supposed to be headed south. I'm following along after her right now. A dancer she knew well in Seattle was killed right after she talked to me. She pointed me here after the cops got through with me. I can't say for sure that has anything to do with your daughter, but I hate coincidences." I let that sink in before I continue.

"I'm driving south and east still following her trail. I can't say for sure she is any danger, but I think it's way too likely to ignore."

He was quiet for a moment.

"Where is south and east?" he asked.

I was trying to keep that to myself. But he was footing the bill, and he was going to find out, one way or the other.

"Next stop is Reno. I won't know anything more 'til I get there and look around. When

I've got some hard information or a location you'll get it right away."

"That will be real nice," he said and hung up.

I was very glad I wasn't Kate's high school boyfriend. Having to talk to Daddy while she got ready for the prom would be almost no fun at all.

I think I-5 is probably my favorite highway of all time. I like Route 66, and I-10 too, but I-5 just gets you up and down the left coast of the good old U.S. of A.

Rooby headed south and I didn't spend much time going less than 70 MPH all morning and afternoon. Sliding down Oregon like shit through a goose past Salem, Eugene and up over Grants Pass.

I stopped at Medford for an early dinner and decided to check out the town's only nudie bar, cleverly named The Office ("Oh, Honey, I'm sorry; I was working late at the Office, yuk, yuk.").

There was an outside chance I'd find our girl there. Besides, I hadn't seen a single naked woman all day and I didn't want that to become a habit—lechery is a powerful force in my life, as it should be in everyone's; it leaves less time for wars.

There were about fifteen pretty ladies entertaining the farmers and salesmen. All working for the dollars they picked up on the stage and the occasional tightly-controlled semi-private lap dance. I looked them over. The majority were white, one oriental, and two black girls that seemed pretty exotic to some of the locals, but no Kates or Salomes.

It's always tough tearing myself away from a place like that, but I got out of there in a couple of hours. I drove on down into the Golden State, making it to Weed by dusk.

A beautiful part of the world. Just past Mount Shasta, Highway 89 headed east through McCloud and down into the Lassen National Forest. It's a lovely drive through the countryside, if you are not in much of a hurry. But at night it's a curvy two-lane with too much traffic.

There really isn't a quick way to Reno, unless you go all the way to Sacramento, and that's the long leg of the triangle. So I just settled in for a long evening and made sure I kept the gas tank from getting too empty.

It was damn near midnight when I finally hit Reno. I know the biggest little city sort of well, so it didn't take me too long to find Fourth Street and head east. This was not the high rent district.

Diamond Dolls was half a block off the street. A block further on was the Fantasy Girls with a nice sleazy motel across the street.

It had been a long day. Even I didn't feel like another titty bar. Just a bed whose sheets didn't have any obvious pecker tracks that were not my own. There seemed to be plenty of vacant rooms. Not many cars in the parking lot. A thin weary-looking man answered the night bell next to a sort of teller's window beside the locked office door.

He seemed happy to rent a room to a non-tweaking sober person. Forty bucks got me your fairly standard bed with a bath.

I was asleep fifteen minutes later.

■ ■ ■

It was almost noon before I got myself shat, showered and shaved and poked my head out of the motel room. The fenced-in parking lot didn't look much better than it had last night, but Rooby was okay.

I've already mentioned my feelings about mornings, but mornings are especially unpopular for dancers at topless bars, since most of their customers are at least pretending to do some sort of work in the mornings, so they could slink away to the bar in the afternoon for the skin show and the beer. Most dancers didn't get there much before noon, so I figured I had a couple of hours to kill before I would really find anything out at Diamond Dolls.

It was possible I'd find Kate working there, all safe and secure and case closed, but I didn't think so. I headed for the motel office.

A plump blonde with a pensive expression on her face that looked like it had been there for a while peered out at me from behind the counter in the tiny office. Just for fun I show her Kate's picture.

She shook her head. "No, I don't know her. She a dancer or a hooker?"

I shrugged. "As far as I know, she's just a dancer, maybe just got to town. Could be a little short on cash, might be working at one of the clubs around here."

She shrugged; it was that kind of a morning. "You might show it to my husband." The pensive expression was back. "He's the one who rented you the room. He's sleeping now, though. Had to kick some assholes out at three in the morning for going nuts all over each other. You sleep through all that?"

"Yes, I guess I needed the sleep. No need to bother him, but I'd like to pay another day's rent and maybe if I don't have any luck today, I'll ask him tonight."

I wandered up the street to a small casino that had a breakfast special and lost twenty bucks to the slots over the next two hours.

■ ■ ■

According to the sign on the roof, Diamond Dolls' happy hour started at three PM. So that's about when I sauntered up to the door.

Stone lions, the kind you saw guarding the steps of libraries, flank the door. Ineffectual guardians of the dancing ladies' virtue would be my first guess, but I don't think I'll mention that to anyone. I've had enough blank expressions this morning, including my own.

Inside, I grabbed a comfortable chair right in front of the stage. A bright-eyed lady with curly black hair, a halter top with rhinestones that spelled out Jizz Junkie, and a tiny skirt that just covered her trigger, as long as she didn't bend over or sneeze, took great interest in my drink order.

"Ever heard of PBR?" I asked.

She looked confused and perplexed.

"Just a big old draft beer and change for a twenty-dollar bill in ones, please. I've got some panties to fill."

She gave me a big smile and turned to the man at the next table to get his order. She bent over just a tiny bit. A black thong—one of my favorites.

After she brought my beer and bucks, I settled down to some serious drinking and leering. I have never figured out why I like these places so much, but since there are a big old bunch of them all over the world I was not alone.

Of course, I have a theory. I watched a Science Channel report on the organization of a tribe of monkeys a few years ago. See, there is one leader, by his strength or cunning or political skills, who has assumed power. We'll call him the big monkey. Well, during the long lazy days in Monkeydom, he sits on his regal tuft, eating the royal salad, while every member of his tribe, gang, cluster, whatever, must come up and turn around and bend over to show him their asses.

Same thing with human kings: come on into the royal presence and you gotta grab some floor and stick your butt in the air. It is called displaying. The connotations are pretty obvious even to a non-animal psychologist like myself. (And I don't even play one of those in any of my fantasies.) Simply put, your ass is mine. I could fuck it. Kill it. Or make you a duke, but it was all up to me. I'm the king, I'm the big monkey!

Same feeling I got sitting in front of the stage at this club. With the important exception, I could skip most of the uninteresting, overweight, or old and wrinkled asses. And all it costs me was a few one dollar bills and beer at happy hour prices. "Dance on," I said majestically.

There were about 20 girls working the stages and crowd this afternoon—almost as many dancers as customers. I decided to watch the girls for a while and not ask any questions or talk to the manager, a slender, nervous man with a Taser on his hip. I had heard Kate was in a hyper-nervous state and if she was upstairs, or in the dressing room, and heard that someone was asking about her, she might bolt and off we'd go again.

Every girl got at least one dollar per song. They did two song sets with the last song done, usually, just wearing a tiny thong.

A slender Eurasian girl, with shiny black hair down to her waist, struck me as completely adorable. I put two dollars on the stage and she crawled over, got on her knees, grabbed me by the ears and rubbed my face all over her chest. Then, she leaned back and transferred my nose to the crotch of her thong, and rubbed it briskly.

Patchouli and pussy might not be the name of the next hot perfume, but it smells like a little bit wonderful to me.

"I'll never wash my face again," I told her.

She laughed and pushed my head back.

The next girl was slender and young. Early twenties with a naughty little girl grin that I was sure she practiced in front of the mirror every morning. She crawled over and gave me a hug, and the day suddenly got a whole lot more interesting.

On her forearm she had the same JRR Tolkien tattoo that Kate wore. This girl was three inches shorter and even slenderer than Kate Hickok—so she sure wasn't the same girl, and this could not be a coincidence.

I put a five on the stage and gave her a big smile. "Let me buy you a drink when you get down, sweetheart."

"Happy to, darling." She had a high, sweet, flat Midwestern accent.

When she was dressed, well almost, she came to get me and we moved to a slightly darker corner table. The black-thonged waitress brought her a vodka cranberry with a wicked grin.

"You two have fun now."

We touched glasses and she took a sip and snuggled next to me with a hand on my thigh.

"What's your name, sweetheart?" I asked.

"Kansas. That's my stage name anyway, because that's where I grew up."

"Well, I don't think you are in Kansas any more."

"The Wizard of Oz. I get it. I'm glad I'm not in Kansas any more. I didn't like my dad much. He was kind of heavy-handed, but then again I was kind of a handful to raise, I guess. I was the high school slut." She had a nice giggle.

"When did you give your first blow job?"

"When I was twelve. It wasn't for money or anything. We were playing Truth or Dare."

I nodded sagely. "Yup, I always fall for that one."

I signaled the waitress with a wink and a twirling finger and Kansas had another drink and I had another beer.

I didn't think the last one was anywhere near the first of the day for her. Considering the fact she couldn't weigh ninety-five pounds, she was holding up pretty well.

"I didn't start fucking 'til I was sixteen though."

More sage nodding. I looked thoughtfully at her. "It's good to wait 'til you get a little maturity, but on the other hand, I've always felt that abstinence is the weirdest fetish."

She let that one sail by, which was about what it deserved.

"So when I was eighteen and this big handsome guy came through town driving a brand new Lincoln convertible, and says he is going to Las Vegas to make a dirty movie, I ran home and packed a bag and hopped in. He had the biggest cock I've seen before or since. And I've seen some big dicks. I made ten movies in Vegas and Miami. I stopped six months ago when I moved up here to Reno."

I put on a bemused look, like I was measuring my member.

"Why give up the good life? You're still young and pretty and you should be at the height of your career."

"I had to get out of Vegas. I was smoking a lot of crack the last year. And I got married after I got pregnant. I have a beautiful baby boy. But I was staying out all night, hanging in crack houses and leaving him home with his daddy."

This time I shook my head. I was a master at interrogation. "That sounds kind of scary."

Vigorous nodding. "Especially when you are the only white girl, trying to get guys to share their rock. I never fucked for crack, but I gave a blow job once. That disgusted me so much I went home and vowed to get out of the crack life. I knew I couldn't do it in Las Vegas, so we packed up and moved up here. I make pretty good money working here, and I haven't had a pipe in six months. I give real good dances upstairs in the VIP rooms." Her hand moved up and gave my fly a friendly rub.

"How much is that?" I asked.

"Two hundred will get you half an hour, and I'll treat you real good." She was breathing in my ear.

"That sounds like a lot of fun, but let's have one more drink before we do that."

She nodded happily. Miss Tiny-thong replenished us with a wink.

"What's that on your arm?" I asked Kansas.

She waved it in my face. "It looks like a tattoo, doesn't it?" She gave me a sly smile. "I drew it on my arm with black ink, day before yesterday. I keep touching it up every so often. I want to get a real tattoo like this, and I don't want to forget what it looks like. You like it?"

I took her arm and studied it. "Yes I do. What does it mean? Is it an Indian sign or what?"

She shook her head solemnly. "No, it's the initials of a writer named 'Token.' He writes fairy tales and science fiction, shit like that."

I raised an eyebrow cleverly. "Oh, yeah? You really like him, I guess."

She shrugged. "I haven't really read him yet, but I'm going to. I'm going to get it 'cause it's like one my girlfriend had on her arm. We're going to, maybe, do some girl-on-girl shows in a little while, when I get my shit together."

I tried to look smarmy. It wasn't too difficult, really. "So you like girls and boys?"

"Not most of the time, but this girl is really special, she's so hot. And smart. She got to town a few days ago and I let her stay with me. My husband and baby are staying with his mother down in Crescent City, while I get us some money together. I'm staying in a motel down the street. She needed some place to stay and I let her stay with me, and one thing led to something else."

Kansas put her lips right next to my ear and rubbed my crotch again. "She has the sweetest pussy I've ever licked." She giggled.

"If you are trying to give me a hard-on, it's working."

She already knew that.

"So when can I meet this hot lezzy girl? Maybe I'd pay pretty well for a two girl show over at my motel."

She shook her head sadly. "She was real nervous. Said she had to move on for a while and work some things out. Leave me your phone number and I'll call you when she gets back."

I nodded and gave her a card.

"So, lover," she was rubbing more vigorously now, "you promised me a VIP dance."

"Let's go, sweetheart." I was getting interested in this venture.

She took my hand and we threaded our way through the tables, up some very steep stairs to a small, mirrored room with a worn couch that was right over the stage.

"Give me two hundred, baby, and I'll run it down to the manager and we'll get down to business."

Her eyes were about two inches in front of mine as she leaned forward with both hands in my lap. She might have been trying to hypnotize me.

It was working. I gave her the money quickly and willingly.

She was back in five minutes and immediately shucked off everything but a very small pink thong before jumping in my lap.

"I get real horny working here sometimes." She was grinding hard on my hard spot.

"Oh yes, dear. Let me help." I put my hand down there and started rubbing her panties.

My, but they were very wet. I pulled them over to the side to get to her clitty. "I'm still turned on by thinking about you and your girlfriend. Where did she go?"

Her eyes were closed and her abdomen started jumping.

"Ooh, go out east to the Wild Horse Ranch and bring her back with you, I'm coming now. Unh, unh, do you feel me come?"

I did indeed. My hand was very slippery and my cock wanted out of my pants in a big way. Kansas accomplished this with practiced dexterity and rubbed it with her own juices. It didn't take long to give me a big wet spot on the front of my pants.

She tucked me back in and we just hugged for a while.

Finally she pushed away from me and started to pull on some clothes. "I loved that, baby. I hope you come back to see me. Go on out to the Patrick exit and bring Salome back to me and we'll show you a real good time."

With a wink she was out the door as I pulled my shirt out of my pants to cover my own goopy wet spot.

I kind of stumbled downstairs to a table in the second row from the stage and my favorite shameless waitress was there in seconds with another beer. Her eyes went down to my shirt tail and that little wicked grin was back.

"Are we having fun yet?"

"Only in the biblical sense," I said. I have no idea what that meant, but I felt for some reason I had to say something.

I just sat there through several cigarettes and another beer. Kansas came by occasionally to rub her tits on my head. Finally, my surreptitious touch told me my pants were pretty dry.

The very pretty Eurasian girl from earlier in the day climbed on stage. I moved to the front row, thinking I would give her a couple of bucks and then head to the motel for a good night's sleep before I headed out on the next leg of the chase.

I fished the last two of my second twenty dollars worth of ones out of my pocket—I'd call this a happy afternoon. Just as I got to the stage and put them in my mouth, I felt something wet land on my arm. The girl danced over to me; her smile faded to puzzled and her eyes widened. I looked down at my arm. It was blood.

"Oh, shit!" I yelled and threw the money onstage, heading for the stairs at a run.

One table went down when I hit it with my hip and someone swore. I saw the thin manager started after me with a scowl as I pounded up the stairs.

In the same room where we made each other come about an hour ago, Kansas lay naked on the floor, in almost the same pose that Amanda had died in. Her throat had been slashed with such severity, it gaped open, making me think, for one giddy moment, of a watermelon with a slice gone.

There was a huge puddle on the floor and it was seeping through the cracks between the boards.

It was her blood I was wearing.

. . .

CHAPTER SEVEN

I stood there for what seemed like a very long time, but probably only a couple of minutes passed before the manager barreled into my back, almost knocking me into the pool of blood. Now it was his turn to freeze and stare.

All he could do was shake his head, tears welling up in his eyes. "Oh, Sarah," he moaned, "You poor little cunt. You sure as shit didn't deserve this."

I put my hand on his shoulder. "She seemed like a good kid," I said softly.

"She was one of the good ones, trying to be a good mother to her baby boy. Oh shit, I'm gonna have to call her husband, Tom... and poor Davey ain't got a mother anymore. I've seen some hard crap in this crazy business but nothing like this."

More heavy foot steps pounded up the stairs accompanied by a deep harsh voice. "Hey, Butch, there's blood all over the stage down there. The girls are freakin' out and so are the customers."

The manager swiveled around and barked, "Bob, go back down and try and calm everyone down. I'll be down in a minute." He turned back to me. "What's your story—before the cops get here? I'm not very fond of cops, but if you had something to do with this I'll feed you to them piece by piece."

There were still a couple of tears on his cheeks but he wasn't crying. His eyes were hot and dry.

I knew I'd better make this good. And true. He didn't look like he'd eat much bullshit. "I never met Kansas—Sarah—before today. I don't know why she's dead, but I've seen a lot of death lately, all in the wake of a girl, Kate, who came through here a few days ago. The one Sarah befriended."

Butch nodded. He was still giving me those hot eyes.

"I think the same asshole that killed this girl, killed a couple of people in Seattle last week. Kate is in great danger and I think I've got a better chance than anyone else to find her and maybe keep this from happening to her." I pointed down at poor dead Sarah. "Whoever did this left here just a few minutes ago. I don't have time to let the cops squeeze my nuts all night. Let me get after him. You might be saving another girl's life."

I was still pointing at Kansas but Butch was not looking at her—his hard narrowed eyes never left my face. Finally he nodded slightly. "Sarah came down to me a while back, after she did you up here. She liked you and said maybe you could get Kate to come back and work here again. She was all excited. Maybe she wasn't the sharpest tack in the box, but she was a sweet bighearted girl. She came back a little later and said she had a live one up here—gave me four hundred to hold for her. She looked kind of sly, like she was gonna do something a little different. But I trusted her more than most of the girls and figured she wouldn't get too far out of line, and God damn it, I was gonna get some head from one of the other girls and kinda let things slide for a few minutes. I might have been able to stop this if I hadn't been thinkin' with my dick. Come with me."

He turned down a narrow hallway that headed toward the back of the bar and ended at a thick door. "This leads down some stairs and through the girls' dressing room, then out the back. That way they can clean up after a good session up here, or get out of a bad one. You'll probably run into some upset girls down there, but if you tell them Butch sent ya, they'll get out of your way. Go get this asshole, and let me know when ya got him."

I nodded and squeezed his shoulder, then hurried down the stairs and into the dancers' locker room—maybe twenty lockers on two walls with a toilet stall at the end next to another door that said fire exit.

A pretty but scared-looking young brown girl, naked except for a pair of pink panties around her ankles, was sitting on the pot. She looked up at me, a little surprised but not very embarrassed—she didn't try and cover anything up as I rushed toward her.

"Sorry to barge in here. Butch said I could leave this way and I'm in kind of a hurry."

She didn't have time to say anything, or even change expressions before I was past her, hitting the bar release on the door, and stumbling down four concrete steps.

It was early evening, a warm and balmy sunset in the alley. I had been in Diamond Dolls for about four hours. My head was a little fuzzy from the beer but that's not very unusual and it didn't slow me down. A little healthy caution did, though. A stone cold killer had walked this alley less than an hour before me.

My gun was in the trunk of my car but I promised myself that if I made it that far I would keep it on me until this whole bloody shit-storm got resolved. I might even shove it up my ass before I got in the shower.

I had about three blocks to go, so I just tried to channel some kind of kung fu hero as I marched along on hyper alert. Naturally nothing happened, which kind of made sense. If I was a homicidal maniac I might not want to hang around my latest handiwork.

No. I shook my head and amended my last thought. Whatever the reason for all this death, it only coincidentally resembled insanity. This guy, or team, or gang, or whatever, was too skilled and too well-coordinated to be without an underlying purpose.

The motel compound was very quiet. One skinny young woman with stringy hair, a face far older than her years, and a major case of the tweaks, was smoking a cigarette in front of her open doorway.

She eyed me speculatively, probably wondering if I could be a source of either money or drugs to help her get through another miserable day, but lost interest when I jerked open Rooby's trunk, pulling out my bag and rushing to open my door.

The bag had my gun in it of course, a five-shot Rossi .38 I bought a long time ago when I was still driving a taxicab. That was the year crack cocaine made its triumphal entrance into Seattle's urban lifestyle.

A lot of ex-Marines are complete gun enthusiasts. I missed out on that one. When I got out of the Corps, I would have been just as happy to never own a gun again. But I suppose this isn't the right world for that. Anyway, today it felt real good in my hand.

I had a shoulder holster in with it and about thirty extra rounds of hollow point ammo. Time to go to war. Give my regards to Broadway.

It took me about ten minutes to check out. The man was on duty this time. No tearful farewells but he did say he would leave the light on for me. Maybe I'd finally found a home.

The entrance to Highway 80 East towards Sparks and the Patrick exit and whatever fresh indignities life had in store for me was about three blocks from the motel. I headed through the skyline of Sparks Casinos and out into the darkening desert.

I have never actually been to the moon. A surprise, I know. But Nevada's landscape was how I envisioned driving around on the moon might look. Stark desert and strange cliffs and hills that made me very glad I had a good road and an eighty-mile-an-hour capability under Rooby's hood. (I try and keep it under that because of the vicious Nevada cops.)

It was half an hour out to the exit and I got there just as dusk turned to dark. It wasn't hard to follow the signs to the Wild Horse and New Mustang Ranch compound. I hadn't been there before, surprising as that sounds coming from a horn-dog like myself.

It was a bigger enterprise than I expected, including a gatehouse staffed with a competent-looking guard. Tall, ex-military buzz cut and a friendly smile. No gun in sight but I was sure he could find one in a hurry if he had to.

"Good evening, sir," he said. "Remember there are no guns, knives or cameras, even cell phone cameras, allowed in the house. Just leave them in your car. Don't worry about security. Have a good time now."

He raised the yellow barrier and in I went.

I followed a couple of hundred feet of curving driveway to a large well-lit parking lot, like you might find in front of a successful grocery store. The brothels were across the lot from each other—Wild Horse on the left and New Mustang on the right.

I did a slow drive around like I couldn't quite decide where to leave my pretty car, just to see if I could get a little luck going my way for once.

Bingo!

At the far end of the lot, in front of a third long motel-looking structure that might be a spare whorehouse (never hurts to be prepared) sat a black 1966 Impala convertible with a license plate that said FISHUN. The elusive Ms. Hickok was in here somewhere.

I parked next to the Impala with my nose pointed back toward the entrance, as was the Impala's, and just sat there for a while, watching the parking lot and the buildings.

Nothing moved. The nicely garish neon of the two houses shed colored light to dilute the thief-light brightness. They didn't reach down to this end very well, which left me in the shadows. I wanted that.

I decided once again that the best profile was a low one. Just another dumb John full of rum and cum.

Kate was, and should be, still very nervous and goosey, so I should try to get close enough to rub her neck and say some soothing things to her before I told her that a couple of her favorite beautiful little buddies were dead, probably due to the fact they tried to help her, and that I thought she was in deadly danger.

Go for it, young whore whisperer.

I walked up the stairs to the door of the Wild Horse and rang the bell under the sign that told me I was going to have to wear a rubber if I wanted to get laid in here.

The door was opened promptly by a middle-aged, grey-haired, handsome woman dressed for a society soiree with a small welcoming smile. "Yes, sir. Welcome to the Wild Horse."

I was ushered into a large comfortable room with several comfortable couches, a large stone fireplace plus many antelope and deer heads trying to look like they enjoyed being here along the walls. The only way it differed from some rich hunter's lodge was that one wall was a highly polished mirror from floor to ceiling with a doorway at either end.

"Have you ever been here before?" she asked.

I smiled and shook my head. "Not here, no, but I have been to many like establishments."

She smiled and nodded her head toward two guys seated on a couch in front of the mirrored wall. "We were just going to have a line up for these gentlemen, so if you'd care to have seat, the girls will be out shortly."

The two prospective clients were your regular white mid-level executive types. Maybe hunting buddies out hunting a little strange stuff to ease that convention-going loneliness. One looked like he'd been here many times and the other had a case of first-timer's nerves.

The lady moved in front of the mirror to give a practiced speech. "Our ladies will come out one at a time and tell you their names and stand in front of the mirror. After they have all appeared please feel free to pick a girl to give you a tour of the private parts of the place. Just in case you cannot come to a successful financial arrangement with your first choice we suggest you keep an alternate in mind." She gave a final small smile and moved off to the side of the room.

Over the next fifteen minutes, nine girls came out one at a time. Each walked in front of the mirror as if she were an underwear model (instead of trying to get you to rent the underwear's contents). They were all very pretty—not a single dog in the kennel—but that didn't surprise me. This was one of the top houses in Nevada and I imagine they did not have much trouble finding willing working girls.

A very pretty young Asian girl in a tiny bra and even smaller thong disappearing between her firm brown cheeks stirred my interest. But then so did a pair of Barbie Doll blondes. No Kate, though, so I nodded and smiled and headed to the barroom through the door beside the fireplace.

There were a bunch of upholstered conversation booths, a couple of stages and a hippopotamus head over the front door to the parking lot. I understand this all too well. Every time I kill a hippo it makes me horny as hell and I head for the local whorehouse.

There was an L-shaped bar next to one of the stages, the one with the white faux fur rug and the dancers' pole. This looked like a good place to rest my ass—the bar stool, not the rug—and I did so.

No PBR of course, so I ordered a Heineken and waited for inspiration.

The bartender was a friendly blonde lady about my age and we were both looking appreciatively at the various pretty women in lingerie that were wandering around or drinking and eating at the tables and bar.

A lot of them had just been next door at the lineup, but that didn't mean I was tired of looking at them.

"I'd say you've got a pretty nice job here." I was being smarmy again; it was a gift.

The bartender nodded and smiled contentedly. "Oh yes, this is a good place to work. The only small problem is they keep the place kinda warm because the girls don't wear very much in the way of clothes as you can see, which is okay except it makes the kitchen real warm. But the food is good and the management is good to work for. I've worked at four of the houses and this is my favorite by far."

I leaned forward a little as if I was a little nervous about what I was going to say next. "Maybe you can tell me. Say a girl wanted to get into this business in a hurry. You know, really needed some cash in a hurry. Could she just come in here and start turning tricks? A girl I know back in Reno asked me to ask that when she found out I was coming here. She's stripping right now down there."

She shook her head vigorously with a frown. "She might get away with that at some of the smaller houses out east. I've heard some talk about some of them between here and Elko, but not here or at the New Mustang across the way, which by the way, was another place you should visit tonight. She could come up here and dance. We have a dancer here in about fifteen minutes. The dancers can get naked here, unlike down there. But the girls that work here have to do the doctor bit and get a license and all. But, if she was dancing here, they would help her get all that stuff. The dancers make good money on a good night. Stick around and see."

I ordered another beer, promising to do just that.

A few minutes later a very nice, very natural redhead took the stage and seemed very visibly grateful that at least guy—me, as usual—was willing to give her a bunch of dollar bills to admire her various aspects. She did four dances and took a break.

I finished my beer and went out the door and across the parking lot to ring the bell at the New Mustang.

■ ■ ■

I skipped the line-up at the New Mustang and said I'd just schmooze with the girls and watch the dancing for a while—maybe take one of the ladies for a fling later on.

The madam/manager was another middle-aged lady with an elegant manner. She shrugged and smiled. "Please enjoy yourself, that's all we ask."

I gave her my best wink-and-smile combo and headed for the bar behind the very large central stage.

There were a dozen women of all races and stages of undress on the barstools and in booths, and many gave me a speculative smile. I got another Heineken. Again none of these people were Kate so I made sure I had a large number of one-dollar bills and grabbed a barstool by the main stage.

A slender white girl with a wild mane of dark brown hair plopped down next to me.

She was a complete ringer for the girls I used to dance with, and fuck, at various Grateful Dead celebrations under the benign effects of multiple hits of LSD, long before she soiled her first Pampers.

She gave me a brilliant smile and extended her hand. "Hi there, Mister Man, my name is Secret."

"Hi, yourself. My name is not a secret, it's Angus."

"No, no. My name isn't a secret, it is Secret. Because you have to watch my dance to find out what my secret is, but it's very entertaining if you are one of those wonderful human beings who tip the dancers."

"You're not a 'tranny' by some chance, I hope?" I am a very open minded guy, as you might have guessed, but chicks with dicks seem somehow wrong to me.

She swiveled on her stool to face me. She was wearing a tie-dyed flowing cotton sundress, just like those dear long ago straightened-out-and-married hippie girls, one of whom might have been her mother. She pulled it up to her waist and flashed me her hairy girl crotch. Definitely not a boy.

I hoped she wasn't my daughter, or if she was that I never find out. "Okay, that's real girl down there all right. Is the secret that you don't do much genital shaving?"

She had a high wild giggle. "No, not at all. I just like it natural like that. I was in a soft porn movie called 'Hairy Girls of the Northwest Number Five.' All I did was get naked and dance around in a park and climb a tree but I got five hundred dollars for doing it. It doesn't gross you out, does it?"

Now it was my turn to laugh. "Not at all. It's kind of refreshing to see natural snatch... and armpits too?"

She raised her arms and twirled the stool around once to show me both her slightly furry pits.

"That's the girl. Well I'm a curious tipper who likes learning secrets."

"Okely, dokely, diggly, daddy. Let me put my music on and you loosen up those dollar bills." She jumped down and trotted over to the jukebox.

The Dead's "Terrapin Station" started to play and she ran up the stairs to the stage.

One of the girls in the bar yelled, "Okay girls, Secret is gonna give this gent a show."

There were some answering yells and whistles and all the hookers surrounded me, patting and encouraging me to be generous for the best show. I began to wonder what I'd gotten myself into.

Secret gathered her sundress in both fists and started to whip it around and up and down her long, muscular legs. And then lifted the dress higher, turned around and mooned me, showing off her slightly hairy anal cleft with a hint of pink lips peeking out. Her ass was very shapely, high and tight. Then she danced off, showing this side of herself to some of the other patrons, who had gathered around the stage. We all yelled, clapped and threw dollars on the bar.

Secret scooted to the top of the stage, picked up a small beaded bag and took something out, then danced back down to the other end of the stage with her back to me. She seemed to be masturbating but I couldn't quite tell. The customers at that end seemed to love it though. Then she was right in front of me pulling her dress up off over her head with her muff right above my head. Her tits were small and cute and pointy.

"Okay, lover, put five dollars on the stage and I'll show you Secret's secret."

I can resist anything except temptation. I threw down seven.

Secret suddenly dropped into the splits, bringing her crotch down flat on the stage, and then flipped onto her back with her legs still spread one-hundred and eighty degrees.

Her asshole looked like a little pink, pouty mouth surrounded by a little goatee that ended just above her tailbone. Suddenly, it pushed out about half an inch.

I was expecting her to fart explosively when her pussy suddenly opened like one of Georgia O'Keeffe's flowers, and something very white and round shot toward the ceiling.

She had just queefed a ping-pong ball right at me in a graceful arc. I caught it and kissed it to thunderous applause.

Secret shot two more ping-pong balls at other parts of the stage, but nobody else caught a ball or kissed it. One guy ducked away. That amazed me. Some people just don't appreciate the Art of Raunch. They should probably stay home and masturbate to a Victoria's Secret catalog.

The stage was covered with clumps of money when she finally stopped shooting those lucky balls around and started crawling around the stage, a fetching sight in itself, collecting the bucks. Then, she grabbed her dress and ran naked off the stage.

As I watched her disappear through the doorway I hear a familiar voice in my ear.

"God damn it. I love her but that's one fucking hell of a hard act to follow."

I turned to find Kate Hickok sitting on the next barstool.

She was wearing a schoolgirl's blue pleated skirt and white sailor top with obviously unfettered non-schoolgirl tits thrusting at the fabric. Her hair was now a streaking blonde brown mix that I like a lot. Do you think hair ever gets confused when you keep changing its color? Maybe I needed to wait a little while before I had my next beer.

I gave her a smile that was probably as much relief as anything else. "It's very good to see you looking so healthy and happy, kiddo. I've been looking for you for a while. We've got a lot to talk about."

Kate nodded and then shook her head. "I think we do, too. I think I know part of it. And I'm glad you found me, but we can't talk here. Too many little curious ears that I don't know very well. And they are watching the new fish pretty close. I can't take you to the back rooms either. I'm not certified STD-free." She held up a finger and shook it at me. "I am STD-free. But I'm not certified yet. But I get off work at about four in the morning and I could meet you somewhere then."

I nodded. "I know the car you're driving. Mine is parked next to it at the end of the lot."

I looked at my watch. "Why don't I go out to my car and catch a little nap between now and then? It's been kind of a long day. And when you come out we can go anywhere you want."

"Okay," she said, "but not before I dance for you. And you better be generous because I'll bet you've got a pocket full of my daddy's money."

"I wouldn't think of moving before the show is over," I assured her.

Kate gave me a very naughty smile. "I can't spit ping-pong balls out of my crotch, but I think you'll be entertained."

She jumped up and headed for the juke box and I ordered another beer and changed a C-note into five-dollar bills. She was right; after all, it was her daddy's money. Well, not anymore, but maybe after tonight I'd get my bonus and happily return to unemployment. Yeah, right.

I got my beer just as the Reverend Horton Heat's Texas country rock started twanging "Liquor, Beer and Wine," and Kate came tripping on stage, doing her best to look like a shy little schoolgirl.

She swung her skirt up to show white full butt cover cotton underpants—she was right in character. I mean, I think she was in character. I haven't lifted many schoolgirl skirts lately, that is, real schoolgirls, so I'm only guessing they still wear cotton underpants.

The middy blouse came off over her head to whistles and applause. Some of the working girls backed me up again and I handed one a five which she put between her teeth. Kate tripped on over and dropped to her knees, taking it out of the girl's mouth with her teeth. This suddenly seemed like a fine idea, so I put a five in my mouth and she obligingly knee walked over in front of me.

Now, it should be pretty obvious to even the most casual reader by now, that I am much more interested in female backsides than what they wear on their chest. But that being taken as a given, it still allows me, indeed demands that, I appreciate a great set of boobies, and Kate had as fine a rack as I'd seen in a long time—neither too large nor too small, with perfectly perky little pink nipples nuzzling my ears.

She pulled my head back by the ponytail and whispered, "One more time."

I got another five in my mouth in no time at all.

She spread her knees to an almost impossible angle while still holding me by the hair. Then she leaned back and jammed my face right into her Camel's toe, vigorously rubbing it around. She had a light floral scent with tangy vaginal undertones. I was definitely getting aroused and I didn't think I was alone.

She jumped up and bent over wiggling her hips just as The Reverend launched into my all-time favorite song he performs, "Do it One Time for Me," the plaintive plea of a young man who wants to have his girlfriend masturbate in front of him. It's my kind of love song. She grabbed those white panties and slid them down to the stage.

In an interesting contrast to Secret's furry funhouse, there was not a single hair anywhere, from the base of her spine to the pink protrusion of her clit. And I was right about not being the only one who was aroused.

She twirled around and gave me the front view, a tiny curly V-shaped patch just above her cleft that was awfully cute.

She gave me a decidedly un-schoolgirl wicked grin and whipped an eight-inch purple vibrator out of a pocket in her skirt. She spread her knees while keeping her feet fairly close together and started rubbing herself vigorously.

If I know anything about wanking women, and I've got a certain amount of expertise in this area, she wasn't playing. She was intently stirring the soup.

I threw a few more bills on the stage and she flopped on her back with her ankles behind her knees and slid it all the way in to the on/off switch. She was getting that look of serious concentration on her face that said it wouldn't be long now.

She came with a high undulating cry that was echoed by everyone in the whole place just as the song ended, and then slowly pulled the slickly glistening dildo out and rolled it into the pile of money in front of me.

I picked it up and licked it to more cheers and laughter.

I was harder than Chinese algebra at this point.

She seemed pretty shaky as she came over to pick up her money but managed a wicked grin and a wink, then said, "I don't do that all the time, but I wanted to impress you. Are you impressed?" She glanced down at the front of my pants.

Yup, I was still impressing right up against the front of my fly.

Kate tickled my nose with her slippery little friend. "I'll come wake you up around four." I nodded as she left the stage to another round of applause and whistles.

Now it was true I had a hard-on and a pocket full of money. And I was, in fact, in a fancy whorehouse. So given my proclivities, you might imagine I would have grabbed one of these lovelies and headed back into the maze of comfortable little rooms with clean sheets and equally clean tits and ass. And, on just about any other night, your imagination would be right on the money. But this had already been a very long day full of sex, death, driving, and beer. I headed out to my car. Tomorrow was probably going to start early.

The parking lot was well-lit in front of the two ranches, but much darker and shadowed back by the unused third house, where I was parked next to Kate's borrowed Impala. The parking lot was also quiet and drowsy. Practically as soon as I slumped over, I was asleep.

■ ■ ■

A knock on the window woke me up seemingly minutes later, but when I looked at my watch, three hours had passed to indeed make it four in the morning.

Kate was standing by the passenger door, so I opened it and she slid in. She was still wearing the schoolgirl outfit with a long black leather coat over it. I briefly wondered if she had changed her white cotton panties, but that was beneath me. Or maybe beneath her.

"Can I have a smoky treat, Angus?" she asked.

I handed her a Camel, pulled out my Zippo and flicked it open but she put her hand over it.

"Wait one minute. I have to fart." She shifted over toward me for a second. "Okay, it's a silent one. I don't know if it's deadly yet but I guess it's safe to light my smoke." She chuckled. "So Daddy did send you to look for me and you found me. That's pretty clever of you."

I nodded and shrugged as I lit her up. "It wasn't that hard really. The scary thing is I don't think I'm the only one who's sniffing after you.   And whoever else is looking doesn't have your continued good health as a goal."

She nodded solemnly, her eyes large and round. "Do you have any idea who it is?"

"Not yet. But whoever else is on your trail isn't far behind me and..."

That's as far as I got with that sentence when there was a familiar sharp crack and Rooby got a long ricochet crease in her hood.

"Shit! Get down!" I yelled and pulled her down onto the front seat, falling on top of her with my head buried in her ass.

Ordinarily this would have been delightful, if someone hadn't been trying to kill us. It was also somehow eerily familiar.

I groped for my gun, which was digging into Kate's back.

"Listen close, kiddo," I murmured into her ass while rolling down the window and sticking the gun out, shooting one round without looking. With my limited amount of ammunition, that wasn't something I could afford to do very often, but I thought it might buy us a few minutes.

"I'm going to open my door. Your car is next to mine on the opposite side from this asshole, so when I get out you crawl after me. Get in your car and get the fuck out of here. If you stay in the houses along Highway 80, I'll find you soon... maybe in a day or two. I'll keep him pinned down as long as I can, hopefully without getting killed. I hope you have your car keys."

I felt what I thought was Kate nodding and putting her hand in her coat pocket.

I kicked the door open. "Okay, let's go!" I rolled out and threw a couple of rounds over the hood. Kate tumbled out without her usual dancer's grace and crawled quickly into her car.

As the Impala roared to life, I peeked over the hood. There was one of those little grey Japanese cars parked in the shadows about sixty feet away. Someone was crouching behind it. I aimed for the tires and let loose the last two rounds I had in the gun as Kate threw it in gear and smoked the tires heading for the guard shack.

The grey car lurched as the front tire went flat. I dodged around my open front door to the pouch on the floor of the back seat, where I had about fifteen more rounds.

My opponent was silent right now. I reloaded wondering why the guard shack was so quiet. But it had only been a couple of minutes. Time gets real elastic when you are so high on adrenaline. My ears were probably pointy.

I crouched behind the trunk and shot a round at the rear tire. It satisfyingly went flat. Not bad considering how long it had been since I shot it at anything. This was not a long-range weapon.

The rifle blasted again and my front tire exploded with a loud eructation; a second later, the rear tire went the same way. Neither one of us was going to be driving anywhere in the near future.

One more bullet ricocheted off the hood.

At least I'd given Kate a chance to escape. Now it would be nice to get out of this alive.

The sniper and I sat like this for what seemed like a long time but was likely only about ten minutes. I detected some curtain flutters from both of the brothels but still nothing from the guard shack. That was kind of ominous. The security arms were raised.

I thought everyone in the ranches, like myself, was hunkered down, waiting for the cops.

With a muffled roar, a long black car rushed past the guard shack, heading for the little grey rice burner. I tried to sling a shot at it but the rifle fired again—right into Rooby's fender. This guy really knew how to piss me off.

But he also knew how to make me keep my head down.

The black car squealed to a stop between me and the grey disabled one. A door slammed, and off they went, out of the compound. I emptied the gun after them without visible results as I ran to the guard's small building.

The guard was on the floor staring glassy-eyed into the corner, his head at an impossible angle. He was very, very dead.

■ ■ ■

CHAPTER EIGHT

All I could do was stand there, staring down at the dead guard. It was the same man who was on duty when I got there the night before. Friendly and competent, I had thought at the time. Maybe too friendly and obviously not quite competent enough.

"Don't worry about security," he'd said. He didn't knock wood afterward. There's a lesson there.

I felt sorry for him, but at the same time I've always felt that if your job is security, well, your ass is on the line whether you're in the military or a rent-a-cop like this guy— or even a half-legit PI from Seattle, for that matter.

If I had caught a severe case of bullet holes, I would have felt sorry for myself, too. But at the same time it would have probably served my dumb ass right.

I became aware of the people coming out of both the houses, seeing me standing there with a warm gun in my hand. I was not going to be able to dodge out on this conversation.

I headed back to my car and placed the gun on the hood. Considering that my opponent had a rifle, fitted with a night scope and all the time he needed, I came off fairly lightly with a couple of flat tires.

I never drive a block without AAA watching my back, and I buy all my tires with Goodyear's road hazard warranty, which would, I hoped, cover bullet holes fired by wacko murderers. So I got on my cell phone for a tow truck and then just waited there for the cops to start giving me grief. I didn't have to wait too long.

The sheriff was one of those tall, thin, mustachioed throwbacks to the cowboy movies of my youth that could almost give me some faith in the law enforcement community—almost. His name was Tom Beekman and he did me the courtesy of not frisking me after he took my gun and studied my ID.

Sheriff Beekman spent several minutes looking at me in silence. This was supposed to make me nervous. I just looked back at him. When he wanted some information I could only assume he'd ask me some questions.

Finally he got around to it. "Most people come out here to play with the girls," he said. "There is a lot of empty country around here you can have your gunfights in without disturbing everybody and getting all the girls panties in a bunch."

I nodded thoughtfully. "I'll keep that in mind next time I get ambushed. This little battle wasn't really my idea. Matter of fact it kinda took me by surprise."

He nodded back. "Maybe you better tell me what you do know, or think you know. You know. Try and convince me not to drop this whole thing in your lap and throw you under the jail."

"Okay," I said. "This is going to take some time. But just for starters you have to know that it was someone a lot younger and stronger than I who killed the gate guard. He seemed reasonably competent to me when he let me drive in. If it's who I think it was that killed him it's a two-person team."

Sheriff Tom was still looking very tense so I just kept on talking.

"The lady they are after for some reason was here last night, dancing her ass off. Well, maybe showing her ass off is a better way of putting it. She had been running from someone all the way from Seattle and her father hired me to find her and help her. Well, I finally found her last night and was just starting to talk to her, to try and figure out why so many people she knows have died violently in the last couple of weeks. That's when a sniper, hiding behind that little piece of shit grey car back over there in the shadows, opened up on us with a rifle that I was pretty sure had a night scope. I was out-gunned by a bunch, but I fired back and at least flattened a couple of his tires and gave Kate a chance to get away. I kept him pinned down until the big black car came blasting in and picked up the shooter and drove away.

"The only way I could figure it is, the gate guard had already been killed, maybe a few hours ago. Then one person drove that car in here quietly while I was sleeping in my car. They wouldn't have noticed me because I was lying down on the seat. I figure the big black car was somewhere fairly close as a back up. They were going to pop Kate and drive away, but they didn't count on me being here and having a gun. So when I flattened the tires on that car it threw a wrench in the works.

Kate shot out of here and the other car had to come in here and rescue the scumbag partner before they could chase her. With a little luck you might find some fingerprints or something in that car and we'll get a name and hammer the bastard."

I stopped for a few deep breaths. As my Granny would have said, that was quite a speech if I do say so myself.

The lanky lawman seemed somehow less impressed. "I don't know how much 'we' there's gonna be in this bastard hammering," he said. "This Kate got a last name?"

"Hickok," I said.

His eyes got a sudden case of the squints. "Would her daddy go by the name of Walter?" he asked.

"He would."

"Huh," he huhhed. "Old Walter grew up around here. Kind of a wild boy, nobody seemed too sorry when he moved away. That girl would be Elka's daughter, I reckon?"

I shrugged. "I don't know the family all that well."

Just then a flatbed wrecker pulled into the compound. I waved him over to the car. "Sheriff, do you mind if I get my tires fixed? You know, just in case you let me drive after Kate, sooner or later."

He squinted some more. He might have had a few too many Clint Eastwood movies rolling around in his head. The ones Sergio Leone ripped of from Akira Kurosawa. "That would be Bill," he said.

The tow truck had Bill's Tow on the door, so that didn't take much detecting.

"Let me talk to him." He strode over to the driver's door just as a short round man in greasy bib overalls climbed out of the cab. "Hi, Bill."

"Hi, Tom." Lots more nodding and smiling.

Tom finally got to the point. "This gentleman got bullet holes in a couple of his tires. Kinda makes 'em flat on one side."

Mutual chuckles and more good old boy bonding I'm not going to bother to repeat. Finally, it was arranged that Rooby would be taken to a Goodyear garage in Sparks.

Sheriff Tom told Bill to make sure they save any bullets they find, for him to pick up later. Then he took me aside and squinted at me some more.

"Mr. Vieira, I think you've been pretty straight with me so far. Kate's momma was a friend of mine a long time ago when I was a little bit wilder than I am now, since I got into law work. I always thought it was sort of a shame, what happened to her. So you give me the license of the car she's driving and describe her for me, and give me a good way I can get in touch with you if I need to, and I'll let you get on down the road. You can climb on in the truck with Bill there, and hopefully keep that girl alive."

Feeling like I had dodged a bullet here, in more ways than one, I readily did as he asked. And old Bill and I got on the road.

The sun rose behind us, as we jolted and rumbled our way back down Highway 80 to

Sparks's Goodyear Store on the outskirts of town.

The manager showed Bill where to put Rooby and then we stood around for a few minutes admiring the bullet creases in her hood and the way bullets could sure rip the shit out of a tire.

"Looks like you kind of lucked out this morning," he said.

"I'm not sure he was trying to kill me," I shook my head. "But I don't think he's a friend of mine. So does my Road Hazard insurance cover bullet holes?"

I sure seemed to be making men squint today. Maybe it was all the sunshine they get down here.

"Oh, I reckon," he said after studying the small book of repair receipts I pulled out of the glove compartment. "You seem to be a real loyal Goodyear customer."

"Yeah, I guess you could say that. It's not so much that you guys are the only people who can fix a Buick Skylark, but I do a lot of traveling and you are just about alone in offering a coast-to-coast warranty these days."

"We'll get it done," he nodded. "Couple of hours will probably do it. Leave me your cell number and we'll call you. There's a small casino down the street with a good breakfast special."

"Thanks. There usually is in this part of the world."

I managed to lose about fifty bucks in the next three hours before my phone rang and I settled up the small charge for balancing.

I wished I had gotten a chance to tell Kate about the messy and tragic death of Kansas. It might've made her take her personal danger even more seriously. But then, that might have made her disappear completely, which might be the best thing for her. Personally, I was deeply angry with these twisted bastards. I didn't want to let them get away with this bloody nightmare.

I'd told Kate to head east on Highway 80 and I would find her in one of the brothels or strip joints along the way. I had picked up a map at the Wild Horse that showed all the houses for working girls in the state.

I made sure the cooler was well stocked with ice-cold PBR (not as easy to find down here as it was up in Washington and Oregon but still available in discerning liquor stores) and Rooby was all gassed up and well oiled. It was a good drive from Sparks to Winnemucca, something like two hundred miles, but I like a good drive.

It was definitely a top down day. Sometimes, a day of wind and sun and seventy miles an hour can revitalize me like a hot tub full of Japanese girls. Well, almost. This was one of those days.

I didn't do much thinking on the drive, just kept my good eye on the road and Waylon, Willie and Tom T. Hall honking out of the speakers, loud enough to cover the wind noise.

I got to Winnemucca around five in the afternoon. The Grove Motel was about two blocks off the main drag—trees in the wide parking lot and big comfortable rooms with plenty of hot water.

After washing the road dust out of my hair and beard, I sauntered down to the Sundance Casino. A fat old steak and baked potato dinner gave me the distinct impression I could whip a room full of tigers. Or at least spank a room full of hookers.

I cranked Rooby to life and drove up the road a few blocks to Baud Street, where a left turn took me down to "The Line," a cul-de-sac with four brothels on one side of the street and one on the other—a plethora of joy as it were.

This being Butch and Sundance country, supporting criminals with a burnished Robin Hood image that you just can't get until a hundred years after you die violently, I decided to hit the Wild West Saloon. The bartender, a stocky woman, who looked like she might like pussy almost as much as I do, cracked me a beer. A slender blonde on the next barstool smiled me a welcome. "We have four girls here this afternoon. Would you like me to call them out here for you?"

I gave her my second-best leer. "So you are not a worker here yourself?" I asked.

She shook her head with a tight smile. "Not anymore. I married a rich man and we bought the clubs—all five of them. I don't sell my ass anymore, so I just sit it in front of the cash register. Not as much fun, but even more lucrative."

I was getting a mite envious. "That sounds like it might be a lot of fun."

She got a wry twist to her mouth. "It's getting to be now, but it wasn't for the first six months. I had to kick out about half the girls for being druggies or wackos. Some of them had their pimps in the local motels smuggling them drugs and stealing all their money. I hate that. The place was pretty run down too. But we are getting there now. The girls are all clean and pretty happy," she shrugged, "for a bunch of single women."

"Speaking of single women," I slid the subject change and a photo of Kate in front of her with my usual subtlety, "have you seen this girl by any chance? Maybe have her working in one of your places?"

This got me another one of those narrow-eyed looks I seemed to be collecting down here in the Silver State.

"Who is she to you?" she asked. "Runaway wife? Girlfriend, you don't look nervous enough to be a stalker, but sometimes it's hard to tell."

I shook my head vigorously and tried to look righteous. That never works very well for me. "Nothing like that. It's a long story, but believe me, she will want to see me and it's definitely in her best interest if I could find her."

She watched me for a while and then shrugged and studied Kate's picture. "She's a hottie. I would hire her as long as she isn't too crazy but I haven't seen her. Is she in trouble?"

I shrugged. "Maybe. Let's just say it's pretty important, would it be okay if I ask some of your girls?"

She smiled. "You can ask the girls anything you want as long as you do it while you're naked in the back room."

Just then and right on cue, a slender, graceful-looking chocolate-brown girl slid onto the barstool next to me and rested her hand lightly on my thigh. She had a sly smile on her face.

"Hello, gorgeous," she said.

Looked like I was going to spend some more of Hickok's money.

When I was on a nasty grain ship, unloading wheat for a month in Alexandria Egypt (and by the way if you ever get a chance to do that, don't) I bought a wood carving of an impossibly beautiful Egyptian Queen named Nefertiti. This girl looked an awful lot like her and I told her so.

"Never titties," she giggled. "I got cute titties."

She put my hand on one of them, while her other hand had found the bulge in the front of my pants. She gave me a little squeeze, which gave her a little more bulge to squeeze and I smiled as I finished my beer. "Let's go see what they look like."

She hopped down—"Oh goody, goody good-looking"—grabbed my hand and led me down a short hallway to one of the little rooms used for negotiations.

We sat in a couple of antique-looking stuffed chairs that had probably been around as long as the house. And that's a long time. Over a hundred years.

"What's your name, sweetheart?" I asked.

"Sapphire, and I'm twenty-two years old, you were probably going to ask that next. What kind of fun are we going to have, baby?"

When I called her "Sweetheart," I was not kidding a bit. I'd seen a lot of pretty women in the last week, but she was right up there at the top. A perfect North African queen with a Valley girl accent. It don't get much better than that.

"Twenty-two is pretty young to have made it out of the amateur ranks and all the way to the Wild West Saloon and brothel. Where are you from?"

"San Francisco. And when you're the kind of naughty girl I am it doesn't take all that long to figure out how you want to make your money. I couldn't wait 'til I was eighteen and could start giving blow jobs to the boys at the O'Farrell Street Theater," she giggled. "Now what can I do for you, baby, to make your day a little better and mine a little bit more lucrative?"

Now in all the mystery stories I read, and I read a lot, the "shamus" is much too fine a person to ever pay for sex. They gave the girl money for information. Fuck that.

I gave her my well-practiced leer. "I love a great blow job, my dear. But I hate rubbers."

She started to shake her head and I held up my hand.

"I know, I know, you have to practice safe sex here, and I am very glad you do, but how about just getting naked and squatting on my chest to give me a great hand job. That's safe and sane and fun for all. Two hundred bucks should make your day a little better, buy you a lot of hand lotion, and at the same time, I'll give you my card with my cell phone number on it and show you a girl's picture. If she shows up looking for work, I'd like you to give me a call. Believe me, she will thank you for it. She might be in great danger from some very bad men."

Sapphire nodded and smiled, then dropped to her knees in front of my chair, with a little hanky in her hand. "That sounds good, lover. If you've been to these places before you know I got to have a look at your stuff to make sure we're nice and healthy. Then we'll go back to my room and get you nice and comfortable."

I stood up and dropped my pants. I've always liked this part of the game. What could be wrong with a pretty girl gazing at your cock with intense interest?

"That's my big boy." She giggled and winked as she turned me this way and that way. "You sure have some big balls."

"They are a great help and comfort to me," I nodded solemnly.

Sapphire had small totally perky tits and a tight hard round ass that she sat happily on my hairy chest. Life was pretty damn fine. I knew I could save a lot of money if I just did it myself but sometimes it was a good idea to get some professional help. And look at all the money I save by never needing a therapist.

■ ■ ■

When Sapphire had cleaned me up and we were, sadly, dressed again, I showed her the picture of Kate. She gave me a great hug and promised to let me know if she heard anything.

"Thanks for everything, dear. I don't think the owner lady likes me much," I said.

"Oh, Aiden's all right. Maybe a little bit paranoid, but this is a crazy business to be in." She shrugged.

I drove slowly back to my motel, my mind still full of snapshots of Sapphire's pussy, to find a long white limousine parked in front of my unit.

Celeste was seated on the top step leading to my door, wearing a little white tank top and white mini-skirt. Her legs were spread kind of far apart, showing off her red panties again. I stopped and stared and pondered. Maybe these were the same red panties. Maybe she only had one pair of panties. Or maybe she had some deep need to wear red panties.

She grinned at me, opening her legs a little wider as she jerked her thumb back over her shoulder. "Mr. Hickok will see you now."

■ ■ ■

CHAPTER NINE

The door to my motel room opened, as if on cue from the Quiz Show host, but no scantily clad ladies with washing machines came out. Instead we had Steve, whom I had met in many venues around Seattle over a number of years, mainly as a bouncer and leg-breaker in clubs and strip joints owned in whole or part by Walter Hickok. We had never locked horns because I am usually not an obnoxious drunk or a horny asshole that requires the attention of the bouncer or manager, so we had generally just nodded and maybe exchanged a greeting or a bad joke. From what I remembered, considering the silly and annoying nature of his job, he had a pretty good sense of humor—something a bit unusual for a gunsel.

Nature had evolved him well for his niche in the urban food chain. He was huge—a very big boy. He had to duck his head slightly to come through the doorway. He walked up behind Celeste and rubbed the top of her head. Which I gathered she liked, because she got a kind of Mona Lisa smile on her pretty face and arched back a little to rub the back of her head on the crotch of his Levi's. He tried for the same smile but it was sort of lost under the brown shrub of his mustache. The hired help seemed to be a happy crew.

I clomped up the stairs past them to go into my room.

Walter Hickok was sitting in the room's only chair watching the soft porn channel on cable T.V.

"No snatch shots and no cum shots make for some very boring porn," he said with a grimace and headshake as he hit the off button on the remote.

"Sorry I'm not more entertaining." I sat on the edge of the bed.

He spent a minute staring at me with his mouth a thin, sour line. I stared back. Sooner or later we'd get past this middle school pissing contest so that maybe I could learn something I thought I needed to know.

"How did you know which motel in which town had my soft porn on it?" I eventually asked.

"Humph," he humphed. "I've got a lot of money and some talented computer people. I'm not very good with one, but the lady on the porch in the scarlet drawers could get into anything. Besides, I only had to look at the towns with the brothels and naked women bars. You are pretty much a pervert at heart."

I shrugged. "You're probably right about that. Everybody needs a hobby. But I'm sorry to have to tell ya, Daddy, but those are the very places where your darling daughter hangs out."

He shrugged. "It goes with the genes. She comes from a long line of beautiful, fucked-up whores. We'll get to that in a minute. First tell me what's been going on? Are you having fun spending my money? Have you run up on her yet?"

It was my turn to give him the steely eye. I still did not trust this guy as far as Steve would let me throw him, but I couldn't see any way to make him the crazy perpetrator who was chasing Kate and creating all this death and havoc. If Daddy wanted his daughter dead for some incomprehensible, incestuous reason, he could have done it during a father daughter brunch, as I had opined earlier, with a little poison and without chewing up all this scenery and spilling all this blood. And I don't even know the word for daughter-cide. It just doesn't seem to occur much outside of the Muslim world, as a punishment for premarital sex.

On the other hand, the pair on the porch could be the deadly Laurel and Hardy homicide team that was giving all this grief to the world. I couldn't think of any reason for them to do that without it being an order from Walter.

"Someone is definitely trying to kill your daughter," I finally told him. "They almost succeeded in doing that back down the road in the parking lot of the Mustang Ranch. They left a gate guard dead in his shack. He wasn't the first victim, just the latest. There is also a dead girl in Reno and one in Seattle. I don't know who they are or why they are doing this but they are, and they are not going to stop until someone stops their clocks, or at least locks them up. They had managed to piss me off like I haven't been pissed in a number of years. So I will probably keep chasing them with or without your backing but the money does help me grease some wheels and lips—and yes, some thighs and asses. I don't know where Kate is right now, but I think I can find her again. She is going to need some help before long and nobody else seems to be standing up."

I stopped to take a breath and get a beer out of the mini-fridge, then sat back down on the edge of the bed and gave him my best poker-player stare.

He seemed a little older than before my little speech, sitting in the old overstuffed chair, scratching the armpit of his Izod shirt, and frowning at the silent TV set.

Finally he turned his frown on me, silent for several minutes, seemingly making up his mind about something he thought was very important.

Then he reached in the pocket of his expensive slacks and pulled a roll of hundred-dollar bills out that maybe would not choke a horse but would certainly take a long time to digest. He slowly counted out fifty of them, stopping to face them the same way, an old cab drivers' habit. He held the stack of bills out to me.

I tried not to take them too eagerly.

"Do whatever you have to, to keep her safe." He gave me a look that clearly said he would not be at all happy with me if something happened to her.

I hoped the look I shot back at him, said, "I wouldn't be very happy with myself if something did." He was either not at all involved with her danger level or he was the world's best actor.

Something Amanda said to me about him maybe being the one guy who could fool me was rattling around in the back of my mind— way back there where I put Amanda. I didn't have time to mourn her at the moment, but there would be time for that when all of this was resolved, one way or the other.

After I took the money and pocketed it, Hickok seemed to relax a little and slumped back into the chair, as though he had done what he could for the moment. He turned his gaze to the ceiling as he began to talk.

"Have you ever heard of Julia Boulette?" he asked, but he didn't look at me, so he couldn't see my head shake. I decided to just shut up and listen.

"I'm going to give you a lot of the background and family history of Kate Hickok. It's something I don't do very often because well, hell, Kate has enough to live down or live up to, with me being her dad and without dragging three generations of dirty drawers out into the street. But if I didn't think I could trust your discretion, I should take my money back and maybe have Steve break one of your legs."

He didn't see my shrug.

"Well, Julia was a New Orleans whore who came out here to Nevada and set up a crib in Virginia City during the silver mining boom. She might have been a little 'high yellow,' as they called people who were less than completely Caucasian back in those much less PC days, but I'm sure that she was beautiful, willful, stubborn and sexy as hell, like all the women that came after her in that line."

I love a story, especially one about hookers and the Old West.

"I doubt if the horny, newly rich Virginia City miners cared much that she wasn't completely white. Hell, after a day in the mines they probably weren't very white themselves. That don't plug no holes, as they say. I get this part of the history from Kate's mother, my ex many, many years later."

He glanced over and then back, gazing at the ceiling.

"And she got it in dribs and dabs from her mother, who hates me to this day. So some of it could be family legend but I think it's fairly accurate. Anyway, Julia got a little knocked up, which given her occupation might have been expected, and came down off the mountain long enough to bear Emma and salt her away with a wet nurse in the railroad town of Elko. Then she went back to work, fucking her way through the army of silver miners up in Virginia City. She was very successful for quite a while. And sent her earnings down to the nurse, who, I've got to say, must have been a loyal and true friend, because she banked the money and invested it in the local businesses, including the flowering brothel trade. Probably at the behest of Julia, who might have figured on retiring there when the miners lost interest in her 'talents'. But before that happened, she managed to get herself viciously murdered by some trick she seriously pissed off. Her killer was never caught, nor was his reason for killing her known."

He shrugged. "However, considering that all the women in that family I've met have an innate ability to infatuate and infuriate a man, in almost heroic proportions, I could understand how it might have happened."

This sent a small chill down my spine that I hoped he didn't notice. He continued to stare at the ceiling as he talked as if this was some kind of a confessional. Come to think of it, that would make me the very unlikely priest.

I didn't want to break his train of thought so I sat still and listened.

"Anyway, Emma grew up and went back east to school for a while but ended up returning to Nevada. Her business acumen must have been pretty good right from the beginning, and this part of the world was booming. She soon succeeded in creating quite an empire.

"Her first husband owned a copper mine down in Ely. He died young and mysteriously. Her second husband was one of those handsome losers that even really smart and beautiful women seem to have a weakness for and a hard time resisting. He fathered Elka—a play on Elko. He was a drunk and a gambler who is rumored to have molested his own daughter. He died of a shotgun blast to the face. The crime was never solved."

He paused for a couple of minutes and then continued on, talking more softly.

"I met Elka when she was twenty-two and I was a couple of years older. I was drifting around the country looking for something to do that paid well without raising too many calluses. So I went to work as a bouncer in one of the brothels. Elka was one of the working girls."

He shrugged again.

"Elka was a very beautiful, very screwy, wild child. Her momma owned the place and was already vastly wealthy, so Elka sure didn't have to suck dick for a living. But she was pretty unmanageable and Emma couldn't complain too much about her career choice, without coming off as a colossal phony. I started taking Elka out to dinner once a week—I did that for a long time. I seemed to be the only guy who came around her who was interested in something other than just getting in her pants. Matter of fact we didn't have sex for about six months.

"Her mother hated me right from the start. She figured I was after her money, and maybe she was partially right, but I was also in love with her, and she with me for a while. Eventually I convinced her to stop screwing for money and marry me. We still lived in a whorehouse her momma owned, but at least now she was the madam. Her mother still disliked me a lot but we came to some sort of armed truce and life sort of settled down. We were making money; life seemed pretty good to me. I was even monogamous for most of the time.

"Elka had baby Kate and I began to think that a brothel might not be the best environment to raise a little girl in. I thought maybe we could go legit. At least move up to managing a casino. Emma owned some of them, too. Matter of fact, now that she was a new Grandma, with me turning out to be a fairly stable guy for a northern Nevadan, we were actually working on some kind of cautious amicability, but you know what they say about entropy."

He stopped again for a while, still staring at the ceiling. Then he continued talking even more quietly.

"Elka started getting even stranger. This was right around the time that crack really got going here in northern Nevada and I should have seen the connection a lot sooner but to be honest, I was getting a little antsy myself. Kate was about two years old and already exhibiting the same rich blend of beauty, flirting, stubbornness and intelligence that her mother was driving me crazy with."

He paused and looked over at me, and then continued with the story.

"So between running the casino, doing some gambling myself and keeping a couple of girls on the side that I still knew from the brothel days, I wasn't home all that often. We had a great big house on the outskirts of Elko, with a live-in Mexican nanny. Emma came by fairly often to bring Kate expensive toys and spoil her every way she could think of, so I was just living the life of a successful, philandering husband. Everything was just going hunky dory till one day Emma showed up at my office down at the casino with her eyes all red like she'd been crying big time."

He shook his head and his voice got a little louder.

"She didn't arrive at a very auspicious moment. She came through the outer door of my secretary's office just as my secretary came out of my office laughing with her lipstick smeared all over her chin and through the open door I could be seen pretty obviously zipping up my fly. She stormed right into my office and slammed the door."

He chuckled. "I'll remember that afternoon for the rest of my life. Emma came over to a chair in front of my desk, the very same one I'd just been sitting in as I got my bi-weekly blow job, and slumped into it. It was probably still warm. I went behind the desk and sat down quickly hoping there wasn't any splooge on the front of my pants and tried to think of something to say to my mother-in-law that wasn't too lame. After all, she was a smart woman who had grown up and around whorehouses since she got off her wet nurse's tit. I should have known better than to bother. She just shook her head impatiently and waved that off and said to me, 'Oh don't worry about that. I've known you were a horny pig, who would cheat on her sooner or later, since way before the wedding. But that's old news; you've got something a lot more important to think about.   And you better not fuck it up, unless you want me for an enemy for the rest of your life.   And believe me, you don't want that.   When was the last time you were at your house with your wife and daughter?'

"Well, I got serious quick.   I had never seen Emma look like she'd been crying, certainly not at my wedding.   I would have bet big bucks I never would."

"'Monday,' I said. She nodded and slumped down a little further in the chair.

"She said, 'Well, Maria is there taking good care of Kate, like she always does, but from what she tells me, Elka left in that little red car of hers pretty soon after you did and hasn't been back since. You know Maria, or you should, and by God, you are going to get to know her better. She isn't very good with the telephone so she just went on with her business knowing that someone would come home sooner or later. She had plenty of food and she is a good woman. Well, I stopped by this morning to make up with Elka. You might not have noticed because you probably haven't seen you wife naked lately since you're such a busy businessman.'

"Now this is the mother-in-law I was better used to dealing with. She went on, 'Elka has been getting thinner and thinner and more nervous over the last few months and the last time we got together, we had a big fight about it. A real screaming match, the kind only she and I could get into. That was about three days ago and we haven't talked since. I've made some phone calls already and nobody has seen her. I'm going to make some more, you can bet on that. Now Walter, we will never be the best of friends, but you have been a fairly competent manager for me in this joint and a better father than most, from what I can see, as long as Elka was at home with the baby, but until we find her you gotta do a better job for the baby. Spend a lot more time at home and buck Maria up. Remember, I said *buck* her up, not fuck her up. You're still the manager here, so I know you'll find some time to fuck around, and I could not give a shit less. Just take care of that baby.'

Walter went over to the small refrigerator and got out one of my PBRs, looked at it with a good deal of thirst and distaste. "I don't know why you drink this stuff with what I'm paying you," he said.

I shrugged and said nothing and he opened the beer before continuing.

"Emma hired PIs, of course, and spent a lot of money looking for Elka. But months went by with no word at all, like she had just driven off into an alternate universe. We didn't get a single clue for over two years, and then it was only finding her car stripped in a parking lot, in San Francisco. That went nowhere."

He took a pull off the PBR. "I am not real fond of anyone telling me what to do. Especially a meddling mother-in-law, but it was in my best interest to take good care of Kate. But more than that, I really got to enjoy it. She was a damn good little kid, when she wasn't throwing a tantrum—then she was a royal pain in the ass—but that didn't happen all that often. She got to me, she still gets to me. I don't love many people in this hard old world but I love that girl."

Another thoughtful pause.

"Anyway, it was over five years before we found Elka."

He took a big swig of beer and looked right at me.

"She was dead. Raped and strangled in an abandoned crack house in Tacoma, Washington. We never found out where she'd been or what she'd been doing all that time, but then, she was a mess even before she died. All her beautiful white teeth were gone, or most of them, along with almost all her body fat, including what used to be a great set of tits. I flew out to identify the body and bring her home.

"We buried her outside of Elko. Emma, as you might imagine, did not take it very well. I think for a while there she could have been certifiably insane. She fired me from the casino job, and seemed to blame me for what had happened to her daughter. She tried to take Kate away from me but she couldn't get away with that. I had made some pretty good money working for her over the years and I hired some lawyers, too. We went round and round, and eventually I sold the big house. I picked up Kate and Maria and moved out to Seattle, where I've done pretty well.

"The last thing Emma said to me, kind of a final curse, was to tell me she'd make sure to keep a good eye on the way that I took care of Kate, and that I'd never see another dime of her money. Like that was a big surprise. Her lawyers sent me a copy of a page from her will that says, when she dies, all her money goes to Elka's children. As far as I know, that is Kate. And from what I hear through some old friends, granny ain't doing so hot. The old bitch might finally be dying. So maybe that's got something to do with what's going down around Kate, but I can't see why. So go on with whatever you can do to figure it out and help her any way you can. You will be well rewarded if you get her back to Seattle safe and sound."

It was my turn to spend some time nodding.

I said, "Thanks for the history. I don't know if it will help, but it can't hurt to know it. It won't go anywhere from me, and I need all the help I can get."

Walter Hickok took another hit off the PBR, made a face like he had a mouth full of cat piss, but eventually swallowed it and said, "You might try and develop some taste buds as you drive around."

I shook my head. "That's not going to happen, and besides I can't afford it."

He opened the door and sauntered out onto the porch to collect his diverse minions, leaving the door open.

I watched as big Steve got in the driver's seat of the white limo. Celeste opened the back door bending over a little too far, to give me one last scarlet flash of her own back door. Hickok got in and she followed. Off they went. I stayed on the porch for a while, staring at nothing in particular.

.   .   .

CHAPTER TEN

One of the best things about Nevada's legal casinos was the fact that if you could control your gullible greed, you can eat and drink very cheaply. Even though I was now a lot better-heeled than I had been in years, old habits die hard.

I went up the street, ate a very good steak dinner, came back to the motel and went to sleep about eight o'clock in the evening. And, with the small exception of a couple of piss breaks, stayed almost dream-free and unconscious until eight o'clock the next morning.

My first foray out of the motel room was to find a branch of my bank to throw most of the money Hickok gave me. The way I'd been getting slammed around lately, not to mention finding relative strangers in my room, it was probably not a good idea to have a big wad of hundreds in my pocket.

I knew that, somewhere, Kate might have her tail in a deep crack, but right now, I didn't have a clue where that crack might be. She still might show up at one of the houses down on The Line and if that happened, I was pretty sure that Sapphire would get in touch with me. I could also go back down there and check the places again myself, but that should come later in the evening when all the girls were more awake, and I was a lot hornier. Gee, I'd developed the ability to give myself a mental leer.

So far I'd been very lucky, if you could call it that, in always being able to get back on her trail. I knew luck could change with a single card or bullet, but you still had to go for the ride or fold your cards. I was sure not going to do that for a while. So I figured I'd give it until tomorrow around checkout time, and then get out my "Pleasure Points of Nevada Map" and get back in the saddle, as it were.

So my day was spent sipping beer while I played the quarter slots in the small casinos along Winnemucca Boulevard.

It had been a while since I went a couple of days without being beat up or shot at, so I gotta say I was enjoying the low key, even non-sexual entertainment. This would probably not last for long.

Slot machines are, in my opinion, one of creation's most seductive forms of reality. Right up there alongside watching a woman's buttocks slowly undulate. There was a hypnotizing quality to the whir of the revolving wheels, or in the case of the more modern ones, the simulated revolving wheels, with the sudden stops that could at any play's end, deliver you a fabulous amount of monetary energy.

Please do not misunderstand me. I am smart enough to realize this was a con game that eventually would leave you poorer than when you started, but then I had been very disappointed by the owners of more than one woman's undulating buttocks, too. So the trick was to use these activities for their entertainment value only. Don't bet the farm.

By eight o'clock I had had enough of this silliness for one day. Enough silly little slot machine songs and even enough beer for the moment. I was about two hundred dollars ahead for once and decided on a small nap before giving the girls up on the line another shot at my fragile chastity.

My room was dark and quiet and did not seem to have had any visitors since I left it—a nice change. I lay down on the bed and was out immediately.

In my dream, I was playing ping-pong with two naked green-skinned nymphs. There was a small dragon under the table.

My cell phone started to play its silly little song and I woke up thinking about how annoying I had always found ping-pong. I've never been any good at it.

It took me a minute to find my phone and I flipped it open as much to shut it up as from any desire to see who wanted to talk to me. It told me it was one a.m. I had slept for quite a while.

The call was a local phone number. A breathy young female voice was already talking to me as I brought the phone to my ear. "Hi lover," she said, "Are you awake? Do you remember me? I'm Sapphire, I work at the Wild West and was fondling your big balls yesterday. Is it coming back to you? Coming back, ya get it?"

I was instantly wide awake. "Yes, yes, yes I do. Yes, I get it, and I think I want you to do it again. Thanks for the call. This was a good way to build your customer base with some of your basest customers, of which I am happy to be one, basically."

This was quite a sentence. I should take evening naps more often.

"Oooo, I'm glad," she oooed, "but even before we get to that, I called to tell you that there was a guy up here at the Saloon that I think you should talk to. He has got a hell of a story to tell that might have something to do with that girl you're looking for."

I told her I would come right over. And I did.

There were only a few cars in the big parking lot that served all five of the houses comprising The Line, so I parked right in front of the Wild West and bellied up to the bar.

A tall, big-breasted redhead with the hard face of a long retired hooker served me a Heineken, looking past me nervously into the parlor. I turned and moved that way.

The first thing I saw was Sapphire's pretty butt, nicely semi-covered by white baby doll ruffles that set off her brown skin like foam on a Café Mocha. She was leaning over a man sitting in one of the arm chairs, talking to him. Her back looked kind of tense as she shook her head back and forth. She sensed my approach, straightened up and turned toward me—her aristocratic African features looking sad and troubled. She motioned me over and gave me a hug. Even when she was as obviously worried as she was now, she couldn't help but give me a little hump as she did it. I love a real pro.

She gestured to the man sitting before her and introduced me. "Slim, this is Angus. He is a good man, and might be able to help you figure this out. I trust him and hope you'll tell him the whole story. I know I can't begin to feel what you are going through right now, but that girl is still in danger, maybe Angus can help her if he can find her, and that would make things a little bit better. You know?"

Slim gave a minimal nod. If Sapphire looked worried, this guy looked like he had just gone through a long succession of train wrecks.

Sapphire gave my ear a small kiss and murmured, "I'll get my reward later." And then wandered off, hips switching.

I sat down in a matching chair next to Slim. He was tall and slender and very young, early twenties, with a tan that told of a largely outdoor lifestyle. Short curly black hair and well-trimmed mustache. He stared at me like I might have the answer to a very important question. I doubted that I did.

"Angus Vieira," I said quietly. It looked like it wouldn't take much to get him to run screaming from the room. "I don't have any idea what's happened to you, but it's pretty obvious it was something real bad. Maybe I can help if you tell me about it."

He gave me a limp and sweaty hand to shake. "Slim Thursby is my name, Mr. Vieira, I'm glad I came here. I don't know why I did; it's just that after I left the sheriff's office it was pretty late. I don't really have anywhere to stay tonight. They offered to let me stay in one of the cells, but I just had to get out of there. If anything I can tell you helps that girl, it would be worth it, I guess. I just kind of feel like my life is pretty much over. Tomorrow I guess I'll hitchhike back to Utah."

He looked like he could start crying again at any second. So, I started the way I hoped he would start if the roles were reversed.

"You look like you could really use a drink. I'm buying. Let me get you something and me another beer before we try to figure whatever this is out. What are you drinking?"

He shrugged. "I don't usually drink much alcohol, raised with the word of wisdom and all. But you might be right. I feel like I might just jump outta my skin. Get me whatever you think might be good. Thank you, sir."

I bought him a double Jack and Coke and another beer for me. I had a feeling this was going to take a while.

He took a big thirsty gulp and started to talk very quietly. "I suppose I better start out by telling you how Sassy and I ended up hitching up Highway 80 eastward."

Over the next four hours Slim told me his story. I'm not going to try to completely re-create our conversation as it happened. He broke down a couple of times. Some of it I had to pry out of him like wisdom teeth. Some of it came out in a torrent like a flash flood in an arroyo. I'll try and keep his voice in this narrative.

"Sassy's my girl. She's twenty-two, I'm twenty-three and we just got through with two years at Snow College down in Ephraim, Utah. San Pete County. We're gonna be teachers in the fall. We decided to just get on a bus and come out to Reno for a while this summer, before we really start out in life. Kind of, maybe, get a little non-Mormon look at the world. Neither one of us has traveled very far from Utah. I went to Disneyland once with my family when I was a lot younger.

"Sassy's family has relatives up in Idaho they visit sometimes in the summer and during fishing season. But we are maybe a little less religious than most of our relatives. We are...we *were* gonna be married this fall."

He handed me a picture from his wallet with shaking fingers. This was the first time he really broke down.

I replenished the drinks while he got a handle on himself.

The picture was of Slim and a short very, pretty young lady with an elfin grin and shining hazel eyes, hugging in front of a bar. I did a classic double take. The bar entrance looked a lot like Diamond Dolls in Reno. I didn't mention that to Slim. He didn't need any more distractions.

"Sassy's real name is Susan, Susan Madsen. My real name is Sam Thursby. But she's been Sassy Susan since junior high and it just kind of got shortened to Sassy and everyone just called me Slim. Anyway, we came out to Reno. We each had some money saved—a couple of thousand in my case. She had about half that. We found a cheap motel down on Fourth Avenue, a little ways east of downtown."

I knew right where he was talking about. I had stayed there myself.

He continued. "We played the slots a little, went to see some shows. My favorite was George Carlin. He cracks me up. We were both going to look for work, some kind of minimum wage crap that would allow us to spend the whole summer there but we just kind of kept putting it off. We discovered we kind of liked beer. We had drunk beer before of course, but not much of it, given our mutual friends back in Utah. So when we found a bar about a block from the motel with big old dollar beers during happy hour and lots of girls that danced on a stage practically naked... well, we started going there about every afternoon. It was called Diamond Dolls."

Yup. I had seen that one coming.

"Neither one of us had ever been to a place like that before. The first few times, Sassy kind of disapproved of the girls—said they were kind of lacking in modesty, which might be true, I guess. But the girls would come by and talk to us. Not trying to get me to spend money on lap dances or anything, just being playful, maybe rubbing Sassy's tits or just jumping on my lap for a minute wiggling around. At first we both blushed like crazy, which made the girls laugh, but we kind of liked it after a while.

"Sassy got to like a couple of girls pretty well. They weren't that different from some of our less religious friends back home really, single mothers trying to get by and make enough money to raise the kid. Not celibate exactly, some of them got a little wild upstairs in the private dance rooms. Some of them played with each other, too, after work.

"The first time one of the girls stuck her hand up under Sassy's short skirt, rubbed her crotch and giggled, Sassy's face got so red, I thought she was gonna have a stroke. It got all the girls rolling around. One almost fell off the stage, but a few minutes later when I snuck my hand up there, man oh man her panties were about as wet as I've ever felt them outside of our motel. That night we must have made love about half a dozen times."

I nodded encouragement, barely remembering when I was so young I would say "make love" when I was thinking "fuck our brains out."

"As a matter of fact, I think it was that night that Sassy first suggested that it would be fun to bring another girl in on our love making for a night—maybe, one of the dancers who liked pussy and cock. I just about fell off the bed. Not only because Sassy was pretty straight arrow—shit, all the way through high school all I ever got from her was titty feels and sometimes a cock rub if she was feeling real naughty—but she didn't use words like that till we got out of Utah. Naturally, I told her that would be great. The very thought of it made me horny as hell. I sure didn't think it would ever happen, though. I figured those hot dancer girls probably had all the great sex they could handle, or else you would have to come up with a lot of money to get them to do anything sexy with you. I don't mean they're hookers or anything, but you know," Slim shrugged, "girls get a little friendlier with guys with money."

I allowed that was sometimes true, with a straight face, considering where we were having this conversation—I couldn't really deny it.

Slim went on. "So we were having a good time, what with a little gambling at the slots, happy hour at the Dolls, and some great sex at night in the motel. It was the best summer of my life."

Here he broke down again. I ordered another round—a big double for him. He seemed to need it.

He took the drink gratefully and continued. "Well, we went on this way for a couple of weeks, never really got serious about looking for work, we were having too much fun during the nights in the motel and kinda sleeping late in the morning. The money started to get a little tight and I think Sassy was getting a little homesick, too. Even if we were having a great time, she started to talk a little wistfully about summer in the West Mountains above Ephraim. It was real pretty there. Sassy's older brother had some quarter horses he would let us ride. We would pack a lunch and head on up there. It's a little cooler up high and there was a pool where we had skinny dipped once, me and Sassy and one of her girlfriends named Roxanne. It was all real innocent back then, I mean I liked looking at them and they seemed to like looking at me. Anyway we laughed about that and decided it might be a little different if we did it again. Give young Roxy something to think about."

He shook his head ruefully. "Guess Little Rox's virtue is safe for a while," he started to tear up again but got himself under control. "Anyway, we finally decided that we would leave the next day and head home. We decided to hitchhike east on Highway 80 to save a little money. The weather was beautiful and the people we'd met so far in this state had been real friendly, pretty helpful and all.

"So naturally, we decided to celebrate by going down to Dolls and having a little more beer than usual—no sense leaving Reno without a hangover. Sassy gave me a little smile as we headed out saying she would spend some extra time flirting with the girls so that maybe we would both get lucky. I agreed enthusiastically. We got there and bought a pitcher of MGD, then we got another one. Since we were going to hitch back to Utah we felt we could spend a little extra money, especially with the cheap beer and all. So after a few beers Sass would sometimes go up to the stage when one of the girls she really liked was dancing with a big grin and a dollar bill in her mouth so that the girl would take it out of her mouth with her tits. Or rub her face on the front of her panties. God, I thought that part was great. So did Sassy."

He stopped again and stared of at the corner of the ceiling. I got him another drink, a single with extra Coke this time. I didn't want him to pass out before I got the whole story. I had a feeling the denouement was going to be very weird. I got another beer, of course and brought them back to the Parlor. Slim nodded his thanks with a distracted expression, his eyes still on a scene being re-enacted somewhere beyond the ceiling in the corner of the room.

I gave him some time. A few minutes later he started talking again. "We were both at least half drunk by the time happy hour ended at six o'clock, so we started giving each other little looks and eyebrow raised the way we do when we're thinking about what's gonna happen when we get back to the motel. Then this really pretty girl came tripping up on her really high heels and rubbed Sassy's face on her tits and said, 'Thanks for the dollars in my shorts honey. You sure are a cutie. Is this guy your friend? He's a cutie pie, too.' Then she sat down on Sassy's lap and gave her a kiss right on the mouth. Shit, it was beautiful. I started to get hard just watching them. We had never seen this lady before that day, she just got to town."

I broke in, speaking to him for the first time in over an hour. "Do you remember this girl's name?

He said, "We just knew her by her dancer name, but it was an odd one, real biblical, which appealed to Sassy. Girl called herself Salome."

I just nodded and settled in for the rest of the story.

"So if you bet we didn't leave right then you'd be right. Salome had just hit town and didn't have much money, so we bought her a drink and got us another round of beer. She sat on Sassy's lap for a while until Sassy's legs were about to go to sleep and then she sat on my lap for a while, kind of wiggling around a little bit. She must've felt me getting about half hard. She laughed. Man, her butt was sweet and hot. We talked a while. She said that she was here to make some money to move on down the road. Said her car was kind of a mess, panties and bras, dresses and blankets because she has been sleeping in her car for a few days—showering at truck stops. Well, you can bet Sassy invited her to come back to our motel with us. They gave each other one of those looks when she said that.

"Then they both turned and gave me one of those looks. I nodded so hard my head almost came off. I don't think you could have wiped the grin off my face with a rag full of tear gas."

Slim nodded pretty hard right then and started to grin, then he stopped and the grin disappeared almost before it started. His face started to quiver. It was like his whole face was trying to migrate somewhere with no real idea where it was going. I ordered another round, so he at least had something to put in the middle of it. He did that with a long swig.

He started talking again, slowly. "We both drank a lot more that day than we were used to. Salome had a couple more drinks, went on stage a couple more times. She didn't get any lap dances, but that had a lot to do with her hanging with Sassy and me, mostly. So around seven o'clock happy hour was over and Salome went to get out of her work panties and back into some jeans and a T-shirt, with a picture of a cartoon bunny rabbit, grinning and giving you the finger from between her tits. The writing underneath the bunny said, 'I like it sloppy and weird.' That shirt seemed so funny I left the club giggling like a teenager. Well, I *was* a teenager not so long ago. Compared to Salome's level of experience, Sassy and I were probably still teenagers. Anyway we got in her car. It's a real nice classic convertible but it was kind of messy. I got in the back and I was sitting on a pile of her dirty underwear. I didn't mind that at all and told her so when she tried to apologize—that made her laugh. Sassy showed her where to go and we parked in front of our crack-head motel room.

"Salome brought a bottle of dark rum into the room and set it on the table by the bed, then gave us both a kind of wicked smile as we both just stood there in the doorway of our own room. 'Come on in and shut the door.' She said as she peeled that bunny shirt up over her head. She has really pretty tits. She headed for the bathroom, which was about four steps away. She dropped her jeans and underpants, turned on the shower, jumped in and yelled 'Yeehaaa.' Sassy looked at me, shrugged and started to take her clothes off. She said. 'I think we have some little plastic glasses over there, why don't you pour us all some rum?'

"When Salome got out of the shower she came into the room butt naked and as casual as if we'd all been doing this for years. Maybe she has, I don't know, but Sassy and I sure haven't. I'd never been naked in a room with more than one person at a time. I still had my pants on and Sassy still had her white panties on. Salome grabbed one of the glasses of rum, handed one to each of us and said. 'Here's to now, instead of then, if we never get to it, to do it, we'll never get to it, to do it again.' We all drank and laughed.

"Then Salome jumped up on the bed and pulled Sassy's panties down. She buried her face between Sassy's legs. I know nobody had ever done that to Sassy before, no girl I mean. I tried it a couple of times, but I don't think I really knew how to do it very well. I sure never got Sassy to throw her head back and start making a whole bunch of really high pitched squeals, the way she did after a few minutes of what Salome was doing. Her legs were straight up in the air, quivering and her toes curled over against the soles of her feet. Salome's head sort of nodded up and down against her pussy—I think she even licked her asshole.

"Sassy came with a bunch of screams. I looked down and discovered I had come, too— all over my right fist. I don't even remember consciously deciding to jack off. After a few moments Salome backed away from Sassy and said, 'Yumm.' She glanced over at me with a grin. I felt a little embarrassed, sitting there with my mouth open and a hand full of my semen, but she crawled over and licked my hand and said, 'I like to watch sometimes, too. Let's take a nap now and maybe we can play some more when we wake up.' The light switch was over by the door. She jumped up and shut the light off, went around to the other side of the bed and scootched Sassy over to the center of the bed, then lay down next to her. It was a king-sized bed, fortunately, so there was room for all three of us. I snuggled up to Sassy. She was already passed out, so I put my arm over her and fondled Salome's tits for a minute. Salome kissed my fingers and then I passed out, too.

"When I woke up Salome was gone, leaving a note with her thanks for the nights sleep. She said we were a lot of fun to play with and that we should do it again sometime, when we were a little less drunk. She gave us her cell phone number and ended it with a heart and a bunch of Xs and Os.

"Sassy and I were a little hung over, so we each had a small hit off of the rum that was left from the night before. We made a couple of jokes about if our friends back home could just see us now. We decided that we were really going to head home. That last night with Salome seemed like a fitting way to leave Reno and we were both taking turns singing 'Leaving Las Vegas' as we packed our backpacks. We left a message on Salome's cell answering machine saying how much fun we had with her and how we should do it again sometime. We said we were hitching east on Highway 80 toward Utah, wished her love and luck, checked out of the motel and headed for the ramp to the freeway."

In spite of the great number of Heinekens I had drunk and how very intrigued I was by this young man's story, I had to break in here. "You wouldn't happen to have that phone number with you would you? I'm real interested in talking to this lady."

He shook his head no. "The sheriff's got the note, and my cell phone. But they tried it a bunch of times while they were questioning me. It's either unplugged or destroyed."

I nodded. It couldn't have been that easy.

He continued. "We had a slow day hitching east—a couple of rides by ranchers and farmers that left us in the middle of nowhere, when they turned off on small roads into the high desert. One guy offered to take us to his ranch for dinner, but the way his eyes kept straying to Sassy's chest, and the fact he smelled kinda strong of horses and sweat, made us a little nervous. We thanked him and got out beside the highway. We weren't feeling that sexually adventurous.

"We got into the tiny town of Lovelock around sunset and set up our tent behind the truck stop, jumped into our sleeping bags and slept real good. We'd had an interesting couple of days.

"We slept kinda late. Crawled out of the tent about ten the next morning. We packed up our stuff and headed for the truck stop and some food—they served a good breakfast for about five bucks. We were feeling real good about life in general. After we ate we decided we might as well hang out at the truck stop and try to get a ride, rather than head out walking. We weren't in a big hurry; we had each other for company and a place to eat. We could even take a shower at the stop. The people seemed friendly. So we just hung out by the exit road to the highway. It was a slow day, hot too. Sassy gave me that look she had at about three in the afternoon and said 'Fuck this, let's get some beer and go pitch a tent.' She rubbed the front of my Levi's and she didn't have to wait long for me to say yes.

"We fooled around all afternoon and in the evening came back to the truck stop, took a shower—we could even do that together, and nobody cared. There was a bar there so we shot a little pool. Sassy was terrible at it and I was pretty bad. But we drank some more beer and laughed a whole bunch and then stumbled off into the night and slept again.

"The next morning was pretty much like the last one. We broke camp and packed up and gave each other a pinky promise that today we would get a ride out of there on the way back home. We headed to the truck stop for one last great breakfast.

"When we came out of the Café and headed for the road there was a 1966 black Chevy Impala convertible gassing up at the pumps. The license read FISHUN. The back seat was piled with women's clothes and a lady was bending over the gas cap in a pair of tight Daisy Dukes. That ass looked mighty familiar—we had found Salome again, or she had found us.

"Sassy ran up behind her squealing and spanking her right where her butt came out of those cut-offs. Salome almost dropped her hose. There was general dancing and hugging from all of us, after she got the cap back on the tank.

"Salome looked like she could use a shower and a good night's sleep, but she still looked real good to us. So did that muscle car ride, for that matter.

"She pulled away from the pumps, so we could talk. Salome told us that she had a little problem that was dogging her hard. She looked at us and thought for a couple of minutes, then seemed to brighten up all at once. She got a grin all over her face and said, 'I know just the place, a camp ground where my daddy used to take me when I was a little girl. It's pretty hard to find if you've never been there. There's a creek that empties into a big pool. You can pitch your tent and I've got a great sleeping bag as well as some money I made by hand at my last gig. I'm gonna buy some beer and a couple of bottles of Jaegermeister—we are going to party today. What do you say?'

"We loved the idea. She tripped into the store for food and booze while we packed our stuff in the back seat of the car. We got in the front seat, with Sassy in the middle, and away we went."

Slim stopped again, looking back up into the corner of the room. I didn't think he needed any more booze right now so I just waited until he started talking again. I got the double entendre Kate had thrown him. It had gone right over his head, but then he hadn't seen her on stage at the New Mustang.

Slim was lost in his memories. He sighed and started talking again. "We drove on east for maybe thirty miles, still west of Winnemucca. Salome—I know that must be a stage name, I can't imagine anyone really naming their beautiful daughter Salome—but that's the only name I know her by. Anyway, she turned off the highway and we headed south about a quarter of a mile. We stopped out of sight of the road. It was kind of like a little oasis, trees and a stream that made a pool about thirty feet across—real beautiful spot.

"We set up our tent and Salome laid her sleeping bag out by her car. There wasn't really room in the tent for three sleeping bags. I don't know how many times since then I've wished we had a bigger tent."

He stared at me, waiting for some kind of response. I didn't know what to do, so I just nodded and he went on.

"It was a beautiful desert afternoon, maybe seventy-five degrees, the sky a fine high blue.

Sassy and I put on our swim suits, grabbed a couple of towels and yelled to Salome that we'd be down in the pool. There was nobody around but the three of us, but Sassy and I had only ever gone skinny dipping a couple of times in our adult lives—you know, since we got some pubic hair—and that was back in Utah, where we felt much more at home.

"So we were down there, splashing around and doing some kissing and hugging when Salome came down the trail. She was butt naked, with a bottle of Jaeger in one hand and a joint in the other. She squatted under a tree right in front of us and pissed a good stream. She gave us a big grin and yelled, 'Let's get this fucking party started!'

He shook his head back and forth quickly several times. "We sure did that."

Slim was getting closer to some kind of meltdown with each sentence. He went into some sort of trance, droning on, reliving the events in his mind. I listened, putting it all together.

They did it up proud, partying the way only the young-and-dumb and full-of-cum could party—the way I couldn't anymore. Well, not very often, anymore.

Evidently, the grass blew and the night flew. The bottle of Jaeger died bravely and a bottle of Myer's Rum leaped into the fray of the hilarious trio. The breakfast at the truck stop was the last solid food anyone gave any thought to, with the exception of half a bag of stale Cheetos.

With Sassy's help, Kate did Slim first. She murmured something about owing him one from the other night and always paying her debts, which seemed to make perfect sense to all of them. Then she did Sassy with some help from Slim.

Around midnight they were all around the campfire they had managed to light after several silly failures. They were all doing the Donald Duck (a phrase I had never heard before that means you just wear shirts and not pants), when Sassy suddenly hurled right next to the fire. With her ass in the air, a spume of frothy brown liquid and half digested Cheetos hit the dirt hard—her stomach finally rebelling against its cruel and unusual contents.

Slim found this hilarious and laughed so hard he almost puked. Salome joined in and this pissed Sassy off. She flipped them both off and stalked off into the dark toward the pool, either embarrassed, or mad, or just needing some time away from the substance abuse.

After a while, Salome and Slim crawled into the tent for one last game of rub the bacon. Slim passed out almost immediately, his capacity for lust or much of anything else finally fulfilled for the evening. He didn't think it took very long for Salome to follow him into unconsciousness.

Several hours later Slim came semi-awake and lay there for a few minutes listening to Salome's stomach rumble. She was lying on top of him. It must have eventually awakened her because she stirred, rolled off and crawled out of the tent. He opened one eye a slit to watch her haunches exit the tent flap. Then he fell back to sleep. He was feeling much less than swell. He vaguely remembered hearing a wailing cry later—he couldn't tell how much later.

A long time after that, the sun heated the tent, making it stifling. Slim awoke, drenched in sweat, with a serious need to urinate. He felt as though a giant troll, with a huge tenderizing hammer, had been working out on his head for several long hours. He crawled out of the tent and staggered to his feet squinting at the hazy sunshine.

He saw a full sleeping bag on the other side of the cold fire pit. With a sudden attack of guilt, he gingerly walked over to the bag, trying to think of some kind of affectionate greeting, to get himself out of what could possibly be a fairly deep rift in his relationship.

Sassy lay on her back with sightless eyes staring skyward. Her throat had been deeply cut—her blood staining a wide patch of sand.

Salome and her black convertible were nowhere around.

■ ■ ■

CHAPTER ELEVEN

I woke up in my motel room in Winnemucca from a very strange dream, sweating. I want to tell you it was a dream because I really hate those stories where at the end of the book or movie you find out the whole thing was a dream, everybody's alive and comes out on stage laughing.

I don't mean that everything I have related up to now was a dream. By no means do I mean that. No, I just had a bad Viet Nam dream after I returned to my motel room from the parlor at the Wild West Saloon, where I left Slim Thursby collapsed and sobbing.

Remembering back, I gave Sapphire a few hundred bucks and my thanks and told her I'd come back when I could manage to be horny again, but it might take a while. She nodded with very sad eyes fixed on Slim. I pulled out a couple more hundreds. "Give this to Slim when he settles down a bit. Tell him to get on a bus and go home."

I wasn't in as bad a shape as Slim, or Sassy for that matter, but I was in no shape to get on the highway, so I headed for my room and flipped on the TV, popped the top on a beer and flopped on the bed. I was feeling helpless and drained. Whenever I have a dream where I am once again joining the Marines, or in the Marines and joining my unit in Nam, I know I am in pain, or broke or severely frustrated. The Bob Dylan song kept running through my head: "...And how many deaths would it take 'til we know that too many people have died."

The answer might be blowing in the wind, but I didn't think the killing was done yet and there didn't seem to be squat I could do about it.

Like I said, it was around midday when I woke up sweating and edgy. I packed quickly and checked out. The checkout time was long over but the man at the office was friendly and casual. There were a lot of fine people in Nevada—they far outnumber the homicidal dirt-bags.

Highway 80 east turns south by east after Winnemucca, paralleling the Humboldt River and taking you to the wide spot in the road named Battle Mountain. The battle was between Shoshone Indians and the stagecoach road builders in 1857. Two blocks off the highway sits Donna's Ranch. I got there around four in the afternoon, badly in need of a beer.

The barmaid's name was, rightly enough, Donna; she had a huge, naughty grin, a cold Heineken and a cheerfully dirty mind. I bought her a shot and we toasted the business that keeps her employed. She clinked her shot glass against my bottle and recited, "There once was a lady from Reno / Who lost all her money at Keno / She lay on her back / And rented her sweet crack / And now she owns the fucking casino."

"I'll drink to that," I said to emphasize the obvious. The beer slid down so easily, I soon had a second one in front of me. I casually asked how many girls were working there.

"We got six at the moment," she volunteered. "Do you want me to call for a line-up? We got some pretty girls. They'll make you real happy."

I shook my head. "Not this afternoon, thanks." Slim's grisly adventure was still very much with me, making it just that much more urgent that I find Kate Hickok. I might not be able to help or protect her from this nightmare but I was intent on giving it my best shot as long as I had a pulse.

I pulled out a couple of her pictures and asked Donna if she'd seen her.

She studied the photos for a couple of minutes. "I don't usually answer questions like that. You wouldn't be an irate husband or father or something would you?" She studied me with a lot less friendliness than she had had on her face a minute ago.

I shook my head very emphatically. "No way, I'm a private investigator, but I'm not working for anyone who wants to bring her to Jesus, or back to the farm—to give up her immoral ways and get the babies back swinging on her tits. Fact is, I'm a friend of hers and she's in grave danger. All I want to do is help her stay safe. She's running from some really nasty people. I'm not sure I can protect her because I don't know who they are, although I've got some hunches. I do know how nasty they are. More than one person had ended up dead already. But if I could find her—she, and for that matter, I—

would have a lot better chance of getting out of this alive—a hell of a lot better than chasing after each other!" I gave her my serious look because I was definitely serious. Serious as a pregnant nun. But I don't do serious looks that well or that often. I'm better at angry, happy, horny or wise-ass.

She stared hard at me for a long time, and then her face relaxed back into an amicable wariness—she bought it.

"This is a pretty good house to work in. All the truckers know they'll get a warm welcome, a cup of hot coffee and a shower, if they'd been on the road for a while. All on the house whether they go play with a girl or not. The girls get along pretty well, too. About as well as six pretty working girls can."

As if right on cue, a very pretty long haired Philippina girl in a filmy yellow babydoll nighty, that clearly displayed her perky brown nipples and removed any doubt about the fact that she was traveling commando (not wearing any panties, to you few who might not be familiar with that bit of girly slang). She came up beside me and gently rubbed my upper thigh, not quite high enough to discover my own commando status.

"Hi there, good lookin', let's do some cookin," she said, with a very lecherous wink.

I was almost convinced to give myself a little afternoon orgasm. I return the wink and patted her butt as I ruefully declined with a head shake.

"You look like a mighty tasty treat, sweet cheeks, but I'm gonna have to take a rain check," I said wistfully.

She tossed her head with a small moue and flounced out of the room. I watched her go and almost changed my mind.

Only after she turned the corner could I return my attention to Donna the barmaid. She gave me a crooked grin. "Maria is probably our most popular girl. She would have taken the wrinkles out of your forehead."

I gave her a salacious wink. "That's not the only thing she would have taken the wrinkles out of," I said.

Donna chuckled—we were buddies again.

"Okay, I believe you," she said, "You're too goddamn horny to be an irate husband, and as hard as it is to buy, I think you've got an honest face."

I don't get a lot of compliments, but that one isn't high on the list.

Donna continued, "She stopped by, all right. She looked like a talented amateur, but she was real nervous. She just wanted to turn a few tricks, split the money and get on the road." Donna laughed. "She said, 'Just point me at some bulging Levis, so I can suck some cock and hit the road east.' I liked her a lot. She's got a future in the biz if she wants to pursue it. But it was hard to tell. There's something called sex worker burnout that is a real syndrome. It takes a kind of mental toughness to last in this game. You can make a lot of money in pretty near complete safety while you finance a college education. Or you can spend your off time with a pimp and a drug habit. The choice is yours. Anyway, the couple that owns this place are real strict about the rules. You gotta get your med card and then your county license. Until then, you can't point your toes to Jesus and pray for the big bucks in this place."

That piece of news hit me like a brick. If Kate stopped going to brothels and strip clubs then my chances of finding her went down to nothing.

I must have looked a little crestfallen. Donna opened another beer and slid it over to me without my asking. She glanced toward the door to the back parlor as she lowered her voice a couple of notches and leaned over towards me until her large breasts were flattened on the bar. "If the owner hears me say this, she'll get a major panty wad going, and that will translate into a very uncomfortable wedgy for me." Donna held up a finger. "But like I said, I liked the girl a lot. Believe it or not, she reminded me of my middle daughter, and *she* had a damn good career for a few years. Now, she's pretty happily married, owns a couple of dry cleaner shops down in Carson City and has presented me with a couple of cute grandkids. Her husband is a little scandalized at where Grandma works, but she has him firmly convinced that I shielded her from the sex business. He thinks I fronted her the money for the stores, but no way, she saved it all up selling her ass. Anyway, I'm getting way off the point and you're in kind of in a hurry. I gave her the name of a place down the road about forty miles, in a little town called Carlin. The name of the place is Sharon's and the owners are Sharon and her son. We call Goodtime Charlie."

She shrugged and her tits wiped the bar for her. "We get inspectors through here sniffing up our asses way too often to fuck with a unregistered girl, but their place out there a couple of miles off the highway in Carlin might be someplace she could hang for a while. I told her to come back here after she got her docs."

I finished my beer and gave Donna a hundred-dollar tip. "A hundred bucks," she exclaimed, "and I didn't even get a cock in my mouth, God damn it."

"Maybe next time," I said.

She gave me a great big grin and I headed out the door.

I had forty more miles to cover, forty miles that might bring me to Kate.

Maybe this insanity would be over soon. Maybe.

■ ■ ■

CHAPTER TWELVE

The fact that I had just hurriedly finished a beer in the bar at Donna's did not stop me from grabbing one out of the cooler in Rooby's back seat before I fired her up. One must keep his priorities and his electrolytes in perfect balance. My bullshit level never falls much below ninety percent and seemed to be self-replenishing. But the beer helps, I imagine.

As Tom T. Hall once sang, "My conscience and my sinuses were clear."

I got back on Highway 80, heading east into a beautiful cool twilight, thinking for the millionth time how much I appreciate the top down capability of my big old red ride. I call Rooby "the couch that can cruise the world," which was probably a rip-off of the book about the Restaurant at the End of the Universe.

I pushed Rooby up to seventy, bunched up my eyebrows in the middle of my forehead and sent my mind back over this incredible journey that might have made Odysseus shit his toga.

It had really started with Amanda "Stormy" Smith and her deep desire to nail her dentist, "The Prick's," balls to the nearest wall. That earnest desire stuck five hundred bucks in my bank account, led to a very rum- and sex-soaked evening with the irate wifey-poo and the invitation to amateur night at the Déjà Vu and my meeting with Kate at the Athenian before the contest.

Unknown to her I was already headed over to the Vu to see Stormy and giggle at the new fish. So, I had easily let her convince me to come watch her get naked and dance around—and if the opportunity arose, to be a bent judge in her favor.

Turned out, Kate was easily the class of the field and if the contest wasn't rigged in someone's favor (and I have no idea if they sometimes are), she would have won handily without a judge stuffed in her lack of pockets. She was beautiful and erotic as she displayed her squidgy bits for the handful of Russian sailors, randy husbands avoiding going home to their wives, and the occasional horny and appreciative bachelor, such as myself.

The contest ended with Kate winning handily, and buying me a drink at the Noc Noc. That ended violently with one dead bouncer, one shattered window and my non-bonding moments with the hilarious comedy homicide team of Brownwen and Lo.

I didn't think I'd be getting a birthday card from either one of them, but I didn't end up going downtown with them to the Public Safety building, so I'd call it a draw.

As far as I knew at the time, this bit of perplexing violence was an isolated random death that sometimes happens in any big city (or small town, for that matter) that I had fortunately lived through.

The next evening I'd been by a couple of thugs and treated to a refreshing week-old urine bath in an alley in Pioneer Square. My muggers seemed very interested in this same dancing girl, which caused some little alarms to go off in the "what the fuck" area of my brain.

They got a lot louder the next day when Monica, the lovely barmaid at the Central, called my comfortably sleazy motel to tell me that a pretty girl in a short skirt had come into the bar with a message for me.

This led to my meeting with the anything-but-affable real estate "entrepreneur" Walter Hickok.

To get to Hickok, I had to ease my way past the scarlet-panty clad butt of his secretary Celeste. Something I did bravely.

After some initial bristling and growling like a couple of junk yard dogs, Hickok and I got on amicably enough for me to agree to look into the disappearance of his daughter, Kate—again, that same dancing girl.

He gave me a chunk of change as an advance to cover my expenses, and the key to her third floor condo in Pioneer Square, where I headed next.

There amid the swirled detritus of a very hasty departure that showed no obvious evidence of coercion, I came across a naked girlfriend-to-girlfriend picture of my recent client and fuck buddy Stormy, aka Amanda Smith. So my next stop was Amanda's place and hopefully some useful information from her.

After some deep probing into Amanda's background, or round butt, as it were, she told me that she had helped Kate take off, headed south towards Portland, Oregon, and a strip club called Union Jack's.

As I left Amanda snoozing après-sodomy, headed out her front door, as a change from her backdoor, I caught a real hard object with the back of my head and came back to consciousness staring up into the large impassive face of detective Sgt. Brownwen.

Brownwen had led me out of the apartment house front door, and showed me Amanda, naked and dead on the front lawn. Brownwen informed me that he and Lo, his partner, were getting rather fatigued with the frequency we were meeting in the near vicinity of the recently deceased.

I must have been at my glibbest and most believable right at that moment, which allowed me, by the skin of my hairy ass, to avoid spending the next couple of days in a holding cell talking to lawyers.

The next day, my hat was fitting a little better and my headache a lot more manageable as I headed south to Portland— the first stop on this quest for the unholy frail, Kate.

Union Jack's cornucopia of booze and butts, run by my old Seafarer's Union buddy Jim Dunn, quenched my thirst for both of those commodities and reunited me with one of me and my cock's long-time favorite pole grabbers (in every sense) Danielle, aka Bridget. She told me that Kate had indeed stopped by there for a couple of days of dancing at Jack's to build up a stake, so she could head further south. And she had stayed with Danielle—I'm sure they found something in "cumin'" to talk about. Just like me and Danielle.

Danielle also told me one of the greatest Wal-Mart stories I've ever heard. Pajama pooping through the always low prices, then she had pointed me south with her large and eternally perky after-market tits.

Next stop, Reno, the biggest little city in the world—a whimsical bit of total bullshit but an arguably brilliant piece of phrase-turning by some legendary public relations flack. I got to Reno about midnight and met a girlish dancer going by the moniker Kansas (real name Sarah) about four o'clock the next day. Sarah had drawn a pretty good facsimile of Salome's JRR Tolkien tattoo on her own arm. Our meeting turned out to be her last hour of life. Poor little Sarah—new baby and all. I couldn't figure out how they or he or she or it found her. I wondered if the bad guys were following me, an idea that turned me into a hunting dog from somewhere in the vicinity of hell and made me feel like an especially large bag of homemade shit.

But if they were following me, they were doing it at damn near the speed of light. If they were ahead of me, following the same scent, but possibly from a different source, that would have made me feel an infinitesimally small amount better.

I still wanted my hands around someone's throat, but at least I wasn't the salt lick that got Bambi into the hunter's sights.

The manager of Diamond Dolls let me get out of there before the cops were called. I owe him a big one and if I crawl out of the other end of this bloody tube I was going to stop back there and tell Butch what happened and why.

The only good thing about that day was that Sarah had a chance to tell me where Kate had headed from Reno—namely the upscale whorehouse compound that housed the Wild Horse and the New Mustang. So I stuck my .38 under the front seat and headed out to the Patrick exit.

There I did run into Kate again, briefly, but before we could do much talking, a rifle opened up from behind a little gray car and things got hectic. The sniper had probably been in the parking lot waiting for Kate to walk to her borrowed Impala convertible for a while. Maybe since before I pulled into the lot.

I wracked my brain trying to remember if that car was in the lot when I pulled in— no luck with that. At the time I was kind of excited just to see Kate's car there.

I thought this told me that Sarah told someone else where Kate had gone from the Dolls. Probably while I was sitting downstairs, swilling beer and waiting for the wet spot on the front of my pants to dry, she gave the information to her killer.

I grimaced at the Highway 80 white line. I sure am a crackerjack detective. At least Kate got away alive. But the killer got away, too. At least I gave her a head start. The security guard wasn't that lucky.

I lost some time because I had to go back to Sparks and get a couple of tires with fewer bullet holes.

My hands tightened on the wheel until I consciously loosened them.

From Sparks I drove straight on up the line to Winnemucca, got a room at the Grove Motel and headed over to Baud Street and The Line. I walked into the Wild West Saloon and met a rare dark beauty of obviously North African extraction, by way of San Francisco— Sapphire by name. She gave me a hand in more ways than one.

When I got back to my motel room Walter Hickok and his strange minions, one of whom was snuggled up into her bright-red panties, were comfortably ensconced in my room watching the soft porn channel.

He replenished my expense account while telling my a lot about the family history of Kate Hickok, starting with her great-grandmother Julia Boulette's arrival in Virginia City's red light district during the silver rush.

As Walter said, "Kate comes from a long line of beautiful, fucked-up whores." That sounded a little harsh even to my ears, but then ol' Walt never came across as a font of human kindness and sympathy.

After he and his posse drove off in their big white limo, I actually got to spend the next day quietly relaxing, eating, gambling, sleeping—refreshingly low key until one in the morning, when I got a call from Sapphire.

When I got back to the Wild West Saloon, Sapphire introduced me to Slim Thursby, who proceeded to tell me the horrendous story of the death of his fiancée, Sassy.

In spite of the balmy evening air flowing through the convertible a definite chill ran right up my back. Sassy's death, I was sure, would haunt Slim for the rest of his life.

I shook my head and returned to the here and now. Put away the highway hypnosis and took a right onto Highway 278 just west of Carlin. Down the road a couple of miles was a double-wide trailer with a big sign that read Sharon's.

I parked in front of the place and an air horn bleated loudly. A good-looking, slender gray-haired lady came to the door with a wide grin.

"When I saw you pull up I hit the horn to call my son Charlie. He loves classic cars and yours' is a beaut. 'Cept for the bullet holes. Come on in. Are ya horny or thirsty or what?"

"Thanks," I gave her a big friendly grin and a leer. "I'll think about the horny and the 'or-what' while I drink a beer."

The bar had about five stools. Not large but comfortably low class. Just my style.

I settled in on a stool with yet another Heineken in front of me. My electrolytes were burbling right along.

I admired Sharon's collection of whorehouse books, maps and memorabilia.

The sign on the door of the men's room read "Eve was framed." I nodded sagely.

Halfway through my beer, Sharon's son, Charlie, ambled into the yard. He spent a few minutes walking around my car before coming in and parking on the stool next to me.

"You want to sell it?" he asked with a grin.

Charlie was a slightly raffish looking gent of 40 or so—slender with brown hair. The more brothels I went to the more I realized how far from the mark the stereotypes are about the owners, the girls and the customers. Charlie looked like an accountant for a construction company. He did have kind of a wild grin, though.

"No, thanks," I grinned back at him. "I think it would be kind of a long walk down the road from here with a case of beer under my arm."

There was a stack of Polaroid pictures on the bar with a woman's ass in the top one. Curious as usual, I asked, "What have we here? Mind if I take a look?"

Sharon giggled and Charlie chuckled and said, "Sure, go ahead, but maybe I should explain it's not exactly what it looks like. See, we have a big old cook who got a little adventurous last week. One of the girls, Lux by name, was having a birthday. Now, she was allergic to wheat, so our cook decided to make a gluten free chocolate cake. Well, it never quite set up into a solid cake. He ended up with something that looked a lot like a big bowl of...well, the kindest and most politically-correct description would be dark brown pudding. The cook threw his hands in the air and said 'Have fun with it girls, let's call it Ass Pudding.'

"All the girls started yelling, 'Ass Pudding, Ass Pudding' and dancing around. Then they painted each others' hands with the stuff and spanked each others' asses with it. That's when I grabbed my trusty Polaroid and asked them all to bend over."

I laughed and shuffled through the dozen pictures.

"Looks like you have some prime buttocks here... even if they are kind of gooey."

Toward the end of the stack, one of the pictures showed a very pretty butt with two big hand prints in poopy-looking brown and an arm reaching back to smear the mess around. The arm had Kate's distinctive tattoo on it. I kept on flipping through the pictures without giving any sign of recognition.

"What happened after the pictures?"

Sharon smirked. "They licked each other clean."

"Hmmm," I said thoughtfully. "Maybe I should stick around for desert."

The double entendres flew fast and furious through another beer. Three of the girls wandered in and out of the bar: a Rubenesque blonde, a tiny black girl and a young Latina. I flirted and got them to point out which ass was theirs. Fun and frivolity was the phrase of the day.

Finally, I got around to bringing out the picture of Kate and passed it around, asking if anyone had seen her by chance.

Some glances I was probably not supposed to see flitted back and forth and then Sharon took on the spokeswoman role.

"Hey, we got a bunch of pretty girls here, why do you need another one? Even if she is a cutie."

I tried my serious look again. But after all the silliness that evening, I was not sure this would fly very far. But I had to give it my best shot, so I got out my ID and passed it around to everybody as I explained I had been following her all the way from Seattle in the hope of keeping her alive.

Sharon's smirk looked very quizzical. "Did you ever see 'Blue Velvet'?" she asked.

I nodded. I thought I knew where this was going.

"Isabella Rossellini has a great line in there when she says to Kyle McLachlan, 'Don't know if you are a detective or a pervert.'"

I was right. "The jury is probably still out on that one," I said.

Sharon and Charlie both shrugged and shook their heads as they pretended to study the photograph. Charlie was the better liar but I didn't know if I would believe him if I hadn't known for sure he was lying.

I drank another beer. I couldn't budge them from their assurances that Kate had never been there.

It was almost midnight and if I didn't want to spend the night there paying through the lungs for a sofa, I had to drive on to the next motel.

The good news was that if they wouldn't tell me anything about Kate, I didn't think they would give any information to anyone else.

I thought if Kate had still been there, she would have peeked around a corner and seen me or heard my distinctively raucous voice and come out to cop a feel, or hit me up for some of her daddy's money. So I got a lot of hugs and made a lot of promises to come back and have slippery sex with everybody before heading out the door to my car.

The parking lot was small and close to the front door yet still rather dimly lit and full of shadows. I walked slowly just to make sure Kate's car wasn't squatting somewhere.

As I reached for Rooby's driver's side door handle, a familiar voice behind me said, "I don't think you have any idea what's at stake here." It sounded like there was a hint of regret in the voice. I started to turn around but I was not nearly fast enough to dodge what felt like the small round end of a baseball bat right on the point of my beard. My head jerked back as the bat's other end caught me in the solar plexus. All the breath left my lungs in what probably sounded like a dying belch as my knees buckled.

From the front of the brothel came a loud explosion as my face hit the gravel of the parking lot and I went far, far away.

■ ■ ■

CHAPTER THIRTEEN

I came back to something sort of like consciousness, feeling like I had just tried to eat Rooby's right front fender.

I was lying on a sweetly floral-smelling bed with pink sheets and a matching pink pillow case, which took me back to Seattle for a minute. But then I was just hung over. Now it felt like a large bus was in my crosswalk.

With great effort I turned my head to look around, careful not to move the rest of my body. My image looked back at me from a full length Oval mirror. My jaw looked like I was doing a very bad Jay Leno imitation and each breath caused me great pain just south of my nipples.

I slowly rolled my head the other way and a studio pose of Bettie Page in a ruffled bra and panty set came into view. Bettie is the patron saint of the working girl. Beneath her in a high-backed wing chair was the Rubenesque blonde from last night. Her head fell back against the chair, eyes closed as she breathed deeply through parted lipsticked lips.

She was wearing a tight white T-shirt that said "Trust Me, I'm a Stripper"—obviously no bra, and because it was not that long of a shirt, no panties, either. Another very nicely shaved young lady.

When I looked back up at her face, her eyes were open and she was wearing a small smirk, and making no effort to cover her nudity. As a matter of fact her legs opened a little further.

"You are one horny bastard. Some big guy almost kills ya, and the first thing you think about when you come to is pussy," she said.

I attempted to shrug and smirk, but both of those things hurt.

"It's a gift and a curse," I said. "I guess I'm lying in your bed, huh? Did we fuck? Was it good for you? It feels like it damn near killed me."

She laughed long and hard, which made her titties jiggle fetchingly. It's kind of nice to see an unfettered set of real tits. Surprisingly, working girls seem to be less in love with breast implants than topless dancers. On second thought, maybe that isn't so surprising after all. They had other things to catch your attention.

The blonde girl parted her thighs as far as the wing chair would let her, flashing me a big grin. Maybe she could read my mind. Maybe she just noticed where I was looking. Maybe my mind wasn't that hard to read.

"You can call me Tricksy," she said.

"Can I call you frequently and fervently?" I asked. I tried to sit up, grunting as my chest seemed to light itself on fire. "It might be a few minutes before I'm in shape for some real hoss-fuckin' though."

She giggled and tried to look disappointed as she stood up, turned and knelt on the chair, her legs well apart, pretending to adjust the Bettie Page picture. She had a very fetching pink asshole, slightly funnel shaped with small folds radiating from it into the tan ring around it. Like most slightly plump girls, her butt crack was deep, kind of mysterious as it melded into her pussy lips. She swayed back and forth slightly, knowing what I was looking at, and knowing damned well what I was thinking.

I said, "Tell me something I've always wondered about?"

She looked coyly over her shoulder. "I will if I can, Sweetie."

"Everybody knows what sodomy is. Not to put to fine a point on it, although it has a fine point, that's butt fuckin' and I love it."

She cocked one eyebrow but said nothing.

I pushed on, "So what did they do in Gomorrah? What's Gomorrahmy? Or, Gomorrahfication? What kind of twisted sexual deviation was indulged in by the Gomorrahmites?"

Tricksy gave me a bemused look and shrugged. "I'll just go and tell Sharon you're awake. She wants to talk to you. And it makes me nervous to go down on guys with big purple hickeys on the middle of their chests anyway," she said as she left the room—still naked from the navel down.

You know, if I was Rooby's engine I'd be about seven sparkplugs short of full throttle. I hadn't thought about what I was wearing, or not wearing, yet. I raised the sheet and looked down.

Yup, I was naked, and my chest and stomach looked like one of those cheap modern art prints you saw on the walls of small savings and loan offices in rundown strip malls. "Purple Turmoil" would be etched on the small plate tacked to the frame, with some artist's name you've never heard of—who was probably sucking the manager's cock.

Speaking of cocks, mine seemed to still be contemplating Tricksy's buttocks and showing signs of independent life—ah, lust.

Sharon came into the room in a puffy floral housecoat, looking like a sorority housemother, and sat in the wing chair. She stared at me for several moments, a small quizzical smile tugging at her lips. I stared back—I had some quizzical points myself.

Finally she spoke. "However you're feeling, you wouldn't be feeling anything right now, if Charlie hadn't had that shotgun real handy behind the door. He was watching to make sure you really were going to leave."

"I feel like I was on the receiving end of an asteroid shower," I groaned, "and give my thanks to Charlie, for scaring off the one-man-gang. He didn't happen to kill him by any chance, did he?"

She shook her head. "No. I wish he had, but a big black car came out of nowhere, fast. He jumped into the back and the driver sprayed gravel all over the parking lot as he took off in a dirty cloud of dust. I think he might've chipped your rear window, the prick."

I grimaced. "Damn it! You pretty well gotta take the whole top apart to replace a window. I knew there was some reason I wanted to kill that sumbitch."

She nodded and smiled a little. "I hope you get the chance. Kate told me what's been happening to her the last couple of weeks. Think this guy is the one responsible for all her problems?"

"Responsible? That might be a little too strong a word. But I'd say he is definitely one of the prime movers and shakers. I notice you seem to remember talking to Miss Hickok now."

She shrugged and chuckled. "I saw you noticed that tattoo in the ass pudding pictures. You're pretty good at hiding what you're thinking, but remember, I've owned a whorehouse for a long time. I may not have seen it all, but I've seen most of the things that boys and girls, and girls and girls, and boys and boys, for that matter, do to... and with... and for each other. I shouldn't have left them on the bar I guess, but the odds of someone showing up to look for her seemed kind of remote. When you came waltzing in, it would have looked very odd if I'd grabbed them and put them away. Besides, you slid into asking about her sideways enough, you snuck up on me."

Tricksy came into the room and opened a drawer in her bureau. She pulled out a pair of sheer pink panties and leaned against the chest as she slid them on, snugging them up and checking all the views of them in a full length mirror. The panties didn't do much for her modesty quotient.

She turned to Sharon and said, "There's a rig pulling in—couple of drivers. They gave us a 'breaker, breaker' about half-hour ago. Said they want a shower and some coffee, but I know one of them. Driver Dan, he calls himself." She rolled her eyes. "They'll be here in fifteen minutes or so."

Sharon smiled and gave Tricksy's ass a playful slap. "Okay, give us a few more minutes here and we'll find Angus a different place to rest."

I waited until Tricksy left the room, then shook my head. "I can't stay. I've got to get on the road after this asshole. He's already got a big head start. Can you help me find Kate and maybe keep her a little safer? Before this I had a good idea who I was after. Now I'm sure."

Sharon got up and moved over to the window, pulling aside the drape. The view was mostly desert... mostly cactus... a few stunted trees and off in the distance, some chunky cliffs.

"Yeah, I'll tell you where I told her to go. I can't be sure she went there, though. There's a bordello in Elko called Inez's Dancing and Diddling. I talked to the manager there, a nice lady named Dyna Hong, and she said Kate could stay there and do some work on the down-low 'til she got her legit status. They have four working houses in Elko, all within a three-block area and the cops and inspectors tend to cut them a lot of slack— as long as there aren't too many fights or complaints."

Sharon continued looking out the window. "I think it's pretty unlikely you're one of the bad guys. I know you're smart enough not to draw them to the place. I hope I see her again. Tell her that when her troubles are over she's welcome here, if she stays in the life. She's a lot of fun to hang with."

I assumed that Sharon's interest in looking out the window while talking to me was to give me a little semi-privacy as I slowly work my way out of the bed and into my clothes—she didn't know me well enough to know she could have stared, pointed and giggled.

The clothes were freshly laundered. "Thanks for washing the gravel off my pants," I said.

Sharon shrugged and turned back around as I bent over, painfully, pulling on my engineer boots.

"No problem. We do a lot of laundry around here as you might imagine." She smiled and I smiled back, looking at my watch.

I was feeling marginally better but hoped there were no hundred-yard hurdles in my immediate future. "I see the sun is over the short arm. Sell me one more Heineken and I'll be on way."

Sharon shook her head. "You can have as many beers, or whatever, as you want, but it's on the house. Then go on down the road and save Kate's ass pudding."

I nodded and slowly followed her down the hall to the bar, and gingerly perched on a barstool. "You might throw a double shot of rum on the side, please."

Tricksy came into the room, repositioning her pink panties in respect to her butt crack, and perched on the stool next to me. She leaned forward on the bar to speak softly to Sharon. "The trucker boys are taking showers. That's a very good thing considering that they'd been on the road straight through from Sacramento. They checked out my ass pretty close when I took them some towels. The older, tall, skinny white guy seemed pretty interested in Lux." Tricksy turned and gave me a wink. "She's the tiny black Eurasian girl—a very exotic treat for a California farm boy. So I'll give them an hour to shit, shower and shave, and then I'll give 'em the big flirty pitch. I wanna make some money—I ain't here just for the company."

Tricksy jumped down off the bar stool and flounced off toward her room.

"Thanks for the use of your bed, my deario," I threw after her.

She waved a hand over her shoulder. "Maybe next time you'll put it to better use."

Maybe next time I would. I turned back to the bar where Sharon was running some glasses through the dishwasher.

"Thanks for saving my ass, and for the hospitality and beer. I better get on down the road before I lose my nerve—see if I can find Elko."

She smiled. "Oh, I don't think there's much chance of you losing your nerve. If I was you, I'd worry more about your small supply of common sense. As long as you can follow the white line on Highway 80, I think you'll find Elko in an hour or so—and maybe that guy who wanted real bad to take your head off and show it to ya. From what I saw of him, he looked like somebody had partially shaved a big old brown bear and put some pants on him. Do you know who he was?"

I nodded vigorously, then grabbed my temples, immediately regretting it.

"Oh yeah, there aren't a lot of different people it could be. Thing is he works for Kate's daddy, and Daddy's the guy who's paying me to find her and bring her back safe and sound. So like that Danish fella said, 'Something don't smell right.'"

Sharon popped the top off another green bottle of beer and handed it to me. "Come on back here when it's all over and I'll see if I can get Tricksy to give you her famous round the world tour. Anyway, I want to hear how it all works out."

I knocked wood on that one, gave her a hug and headed slowly out to my car.

Rooby had a couple of non-threatening shotgun pellet gouges in her hood, next to the bullet furrows from the parking lot at the Wild Horse Ranch. This did not lighten my mood.

My .38 revolver left me in that parking lot, too—in an evidence bag in the Sheriff's car. I miss it a lot.

Nevada is a very easy place to buy a gun. If I had any of that common sense Sharon was talking about, I would go and get one. Hell, maybe two. Maybe one of those Buntline Specials, like my boyhood idol Hugh O'Brian wore when he played Wyatt Earp in the fifties television show.

I thought about it as I popped the trunk lid and rummaged around until I found the black steel tube of my cane. I pulled it out, gave it a brief wipe on my pants before giving it a quick inspection. I like a good sword. This one is one of my favorites. I bought it through a sword and knife catalogue several years ago and while I have never cut, stuck, or even threatened anybody with it, it had always seemed to me to have a large supply of intrinsic mayhem in its simple design. The silver cobra head, with its glittering carbuncle eyes, unscrews from the black barrel of the cane and a narrow twenty-inch stainless-steel blade slid out—sharp, good steel, ready for action. It had been in the trunk of my car for a couple of years and there wasn't a spot of rust on it. I laid the cane beside me on the front seat.

I also have a good sharp flick-open switchblade I bought a long time ago in Patya Beach, Thailand. That's pretty much it, though...no guns, no grenades or flame throwers. I gazed at the sky for a moment pondering whether or not I was doing something really stupid. I nodded emphatically that I was, and immediately regretted it, as both my jaw and chest flared up, _emphatically_.

With that, I decided I might as well just get on with it but vowed I'd skip nodding in agreement with myself. After all, I had a hunch I was going to accrue some more aches and pains before this was over with.

I finished the green bottle beer and deposited the empty into an empty PBR box in the back seat, making a mental note that there were only two left in the cooler with a little ice and a lot of water. I'd stop for gas and beer at the first chance I got.

I am not a very introspective person, but even I noted that while I couldn't make time to stop and buy a gun I could easily make time to buy beer. I seemed to have my priorities on straight.

I got in the car and drove back up Highway 278, grabbed a right on to Highway 80, and went straight on to Elko under the balmy sunshine.

Elko was a good-sized town. Easily the largest since I left Sparks. As was the case with a lot of Nevada highway towns, the road was also the town's main street. So I drove slowly up the road, looking for a good cheap motel within walking distance of the small red-light district. Sharon gave me directions to Inez's so I figured I'd settle in and saunter over there later.

My first priority was Kate's safety. I'd clue her in to Walter's murderous perfidy and then go after him, Steve and Celeste, as well as the fucking horse they rode in on. Someday soon I had to stop grinding my teeth—but not today.

I drove past the large hotel casino that was two blocks from the brothels, then another half mile or so further, to the east end of town, before turning around. There was a small grove of trees with a collection of motel cottages on the north side of the street called the Shady Side Bungalows. I looked it over closely—I like single detached rooms. You don't have to be quite as involved with your neighbor's choice in music and sexual proclivities that way. So I pulled in.

I cruised the parking lot before pulling up to the office, looking for anything familiar. Suddenly the hair stood up on the back of my neck. Sitting in front of the furthest unit from the highway was a familiar stretch white limo with Washington plates.

I stopped and stared at it for a few minutes, letting Rooby idle while I finished my beer. I felt the heat of a deep flush spread up from my neck.

I pulled Rooby up in front of the limo, blocking it in. I jumped out with my sword cane in my hand and quickly stepped up onto the porch.

The door was ajar—it might have been a trap, but right then I was several clicks beyond caring. I kicked the door open.

Walter Hickok was sitting in an armchair facing the television, playing what seemed to be the same soft porn movie he found so boring in my room back in Winnemucca. His shirt was unbuttoned and his pants were around his knees.

Walter's head was thrown back against the chair and he had a very surprised expression on his face, along with a gaping gash across his throat, stretching from ear to ear.

I now knew exactly what Shakespeare meant about the old man being so full of blood.

■ ■ ■

CHAPTER FOURTEEN

I stood very still. It was a regular sized standard motel room. So, it was easy to see we were alone, unless someone was hiding in the bathtub or under the bed. But to check that out I would have to go stomping through the congealed puddle of what used to be Walter Hickok's life blood.

I pushed the sword back in its cane scabbard and screwed it shut, then stood staring in to Walter's dead green eyes, looking for some kind of enlightenment. Not a wise-ass jaded comment about soft core porn, but some possible reason why he ended up very dead in a motel room in Elko, with his bloodless, withered dick on display.

This was the third throat slashing in the last week. I remembered Amanda's wound. It looked very similar to this one. I would be willing to make a grisly bet that the same hand—hell, the same knife—caused both deaths. I didn't see the wound that drained Sassy of life, but it would be too much of a coincidence if we had two throat-slashers running around killing people and leaving them for me to stumble on.

Walter was probably many things, some of them less than pleasant, but a fool wasn't one of them. I doubt very much if a stranger could catch him with his pants down and kill him. I didn't care how sexy the killer might be, Daddy Hickok had been around the block way too many times for that to happen. All of which kind of narrowed the pool of usual suspects down.

I wondered if Celeste got any blood on her red panties. My best bet would be she didn't because she was naked when she did it. I pictured her turning the TV on to the porn channel and wrapping her lips around Walter's dick. I think I could safely say she was probably a very proficient cocksucker. I hoped she made him come like a freight train. Then she would have jumped up with a hand to her mouth, like she was about to gag, and headed for the bathroom. Somewhere close by, she would have stashed her knife, or more likely a razor. He might have already had his head thrown back, if not, it would only have taken a quick tug and slash—one cold bitch, this one.

There was not a doubt in my mind that's how it went. And there was not a doubt in my mind that I'd never be able to prove it. She wouldn't have left a single fingerprint. And she would have made some excuse, maybe a bodily function, to get Walter to do the motel check-in.

And while all of that was going down, Steve, of course, was up the road attempting to fracture my jaw and crush my skull—a busy day for the not-so-trusty minions. None of which I could prove.

So seeing as she probably didn't even leave a single pubic hair behind, when the cops showed up and went looking for a suspect... well, the wild-eyed guy with the sword cane in his hand, glaring down at the body, might make a very handy scapegoat. And, seeing as how not too many small town policemen have a very energetic work ethic, it made sense to get my ass out of there.

I've never spent a lot of time worrying about what happens to our "soul" or essence. Archy the cockroach waxed poetically about the transmogrification of the soul down the ages—Mehitabel being a less-than-perfect example.

I suppose that it's possible that an innocent soul weighs less than an angel's cunt-hair. If that's the case, Mr. Hickok's immortal morsel would probably tip the scales somewhere around the same tonnage as a coastwise oil tanker. But I still didn't like what happened to him. It was a shitty way to die. Giving you just enough time on the way out to realize how stupid you were to feed this pretty little pit viper all this time. And he *was* a client. My record has a few small skid marks on it, too. But I didn't like someone getting killed on my watch.

Time to get the hell out of here before the killer dropped a dime on me.

My next stop would be a local gun shop. I was beginning to feel like the only guy in the parade without his pants on. My sword cane was a dandy weapon and if I was lucky, would provide a small surprise factor. But I'd rather not get close enough to big Steve again to find out how thick his skin was. The thought of standing back about twenty feet and sending three or four .38 slugs right dead center into his body mass seemed almost sensual.

I nudged open the door with my foot and closed it again with my hand inside a discretely held handkerchief.

The parking lot was still and quiet. So quiet, Rooby's engine seemed louder than usual as I fired her up and headed out a side entrance onto the highway fronting the motel.

I got in the slow lane, looking for one of those big red signs that said "Guns and Ammo." They were not shy about them down here in cowboy land.

A large black sedan cruised by me in the left lane, going faster than I was by about ten miles an hour. The windows were heavily tinted, but I knew it had to be Steve. He had to have been watching the motel, waiting to finish what he started back at Sharon's. I should have pulled off onto a side street and headed for the nearest cop shop, but there was no reason for them to believe me now, any more than they would have ten minutes before. By then Steve would have been long gone and I was not going to let that happen.

Yes, I should have bought that gun the day before yesterday. I've always liked that line of Red Buttons in "The Bridges of Toko-Ri." He said, "If my momma had only given birth to a girl, I wouldn't be here now." Not much sense in worrying about how I got here. It was way too late for that. Sure I knew it was a trap. But I just wanted to see whose dick ended up in the metal teeth.

The sedan pulled into the lane in front of me and sped up to about fifty. I let it get a few car lengths ahead and matched its speed.

We headed out east of town toward Wells. One of Donna's whorehouses and another called Bella's were out this way, but we didn't go nearly that far. About twenty miles into the brown rocky landscape, the sedan turned south onto a barely visible dirt track. If I was right and it was Steve, he obviously knew where he was going—no doubt, someplace nice and private where we could settle this once and for all. I was sure both of us wouldn't be driving back out again.

If we could have gotten word of this back to a Reno Sports Book, I think old Steve would have been the odds-on favorite, and I wasn't sure I would have put much money on me.

All I had to do was slam on the brakes, flip a U-turn and gun it, letting Rooby bust my ass out of here—right into the arms of the law. Anyway, my Norwegian ancestors were kind of famous for their berserker skills. Not their common sense.

I pulled up to about thirty feet behind the sedan and then backed off a ways. No sense eating any more dust than I had to. That might be quite a lot as it was.

About three miles from the highway the sedan slowed and stopped. I stopped about a hundred feet behind it, shut Rooby down, and waited for Steve to make his next move. I'd spent quite a lot of time lately waiting for his next move one way or the other.

The sedan's driver door opened and Steve's long, very large leg stretched out, almost languidly, wearing a black cowboy boot with a shiny silver tip and tight new-looking black Levi's. I seemed to have had all the time in the world to notice these things—the world had moved into slow motion mode.

Steve stepped out of the car, wearing a white wife-beater and a low-slung gun belt and holster, holding what looked like a very large, shiny revolver.

Things were not looking particularly healthy for my team.

I opened the door and stepped out onto the sand holding my sword cane, which was suddenly beginning to feel as inadequate as Seattle's obese mayor's dick.

I leaned against Rooby's warm fender and watched Steve as I twirled my cane—not in any particular hurry to start this dust-up. Hoyt Axton's ditty about the guy who brought the knife to the gun fight kept running through my head.

Steve, a large, bright grin on his face, pulled the pistol out and twirled it around his thick finger. "I'm starting to like this crazy state," he chuckled. He was obviously having a good time. "Is that one of those sword canes? You planning on me letting my guard down enough for you to stab my big white ass?"

There went that element of surprise. My optimism was really starting to falter. I had left the keys in my ignition. I could still jump in Rooby and try to get out of here, but that hand-cannon looked like it could take my head off right at the shoulders. Besides, the cops were still waiting back in town.

"See this gun?" Steve said. "It's a fairly exact replica of James Butler Hickok's six-shooter. I got the 1860 Army Colt Model 'cause it's got the bigger handle, 'cause I got really big hands. Chambered for .44 ammo—should blow a great big hole right in the middle of your chest. Old Wild Bill... I wonder if he really was related to Walter. I asked him once. He said he didn't know or give a fuck." Steve laughed. "I'll bet he was. The way those Hickoks fuck they could populate the whole state all by themselves."

"He won't be fucking anybody else," I gritted out.

He stopped laughing and shook his head in exasperation.

I started walking slowly toward Steve—no sense putting it off all day, whatever was going to happen. Plus, I wanted to get a closer look at his eyes.

Steve lowered his voice. "He had to die. The Boss had to die. Cee Cee did it. She said it was really easy, considering he was supposed to be so sharp and street smart. Turned out he was just another horny, lonely old fuck. He had to die, and so do you, my friend."

I edged closer as Steve continued to convince me this was the way things had to be.

"No hard feelings," Steve droned on. "Fact is I kind of like you. Kind of always admired the way the girls all seem to like you. And I never had to throw you out of a club for being a drunk asshole. Like I said back at the whorehouse parking lot, you just don't understand what's at stake here. Fact is, that dickhead with the shotgun cost you your life. If he'd minded his own business, I was just going to cripple you up real good. Get you out of action for six months or a year. Long enough to get the will probated and get the lawyers buzzing around."

I stopped walking twenty feet from the back fender of the sedan when I saw his eyes narrow slightly and his right hand twitch a little over that holster holding the hog-leg.

"You ever watch 'Gunsmoke' on the TV Land channel?" he asked.

I nodded. "I'm old enough to remember it on real black and white TV back in my virginal youth, and that was quite a while ago."

There was something very surreal about this whole conversation. Well, welcome to my life, or what remained of it.

Steve fondled the white bone handle of his gun. "My favorite part was when old James Arness would come out at the start of each show and just stand there squinting into the sun. A real stand-up guy, waiting for the other guy to make his move—and then he'd blow his shit away." He shook his head fondly at the memory. "I always wanted to see if I had the balls to do that."

A chill ran down my back as I saw where this was going. I thought old Steve was starting to unravel a little bit. I pulled my shirt out of my pants and pulled it over my head, switching the cane from hand to hand as I did it. I slowly turned around one time. "Steve, I'm not packin'."

Steve stared at my belly and chest the way an artist would look at a half finished project.

"I colored you up pretty good already didn't I?" he smirked.

He really had a very unpleasant smirk that I would have loved to wipe off his face, as the saying goes. But right now it looked more likely that he'd get to smirk down on the buzzard bait that was my next career move.

He shrugged. "Look, my momma is real sick. It ain't an excuse; it's just a no-bullshit situation. This gig will get me a million dollars. I need the money. And I'm also kind of in love with the girl, even though I'm smart enough to know what a cold hearted bitch she is."

I kept slowly turning the cane in my hands. It was coming into focus. "We're talking about Celeste here, I guess. Just how is she gonna get her hands on Kate's grandmother's money? That makes less sense than Walter trying to get the bucks."

He smiled again. I supposed it was better to keep him smiling. I would think it was hard to kill someone you were smiling at. But that's just a theory.

"Celeste is Kate's little sister, you dumb fuck," he said softly. "When Elka took off and tried to suck all the crack in California up her ass, she got knocked up about a year into her drug run at a crack house in the Tenderloin. I'm sure she couldn't have narrowed down who the father was to less than a couple dozen pimps and druggies. Celeste got taken away from her when she was about six months old, and Momma got herself busted for prostitution. She was a classic crack baby, made her way up through the foster home system. And believe me, being a beautiful little girl wasn't always a plus. She sucked her first dick before she was eight years old. Almost like the old joke about the girl that was ate before she was seven. She never found pedophile jokes all that funny. But that might be why she's such a tough and crazy cunt." He shrugged. "But she can be funny and gentle too, to me anyway. And she can suck a golf ball through a garden hose."

I thought I'd have to take his word for that. "So Kate has to be dead before Granny Emma shits the bed for Celeste to get all the money?"

Steve nodded thoughtfully. "Nobody knows yet that Celeste is her granddaughter. She got curious a few years ago and started researching who her mother was. Found out how she died and where her family was from. Found out about the fortune and decided to kind of sneak up on it. She was living in San Francisco shaking her ass at the strip clubs. So it wasn't too much of a stretch for her to move to Seattle and start dancing in Walter's clubs. She's got those legs that go all the way up and make a perfect ass of themselves.

And those trademark red panties... Well, it didn't take too long for that old horndog Walter to notice her. She snuggled right up to him and stuck her hand in his pants." He shrugged. "I already worked for him and it didn't take too long for her to get in my pants, too. Hell, she's beautiful and I'm lonely and horny. We kept it real quiet, so we wouldn't lose our jobs. She needed a lot more fucking than Hickok was giving her. So between us, we knew everything that was going on in his empire. As long as Grandma was healthy we just kept on keeping on. Then a few months ago, one of Walter's spies in Nevada passed him the word that the old bitch had one foot in the grave and the other on that banana peel. Celeste decided to get her ass in gear, but real stealthy-like. It's a sure bet that Emma has someone keeping an eye on her granddaughter. So if Kate got herself killed maybe the will gets changed so that she leaves everything to her pussycat. Who knows? Finally, Cee Cee told me it was time to pull the trigger. I never claimed I was the brains of the outfit. She's got the brains, and the beauty. I'm the muscle. Come to think about it, she's probably meaner than I am. She sure has killed more people in the last couple of weeks than I have."

"But you were the one who drilled Brian and the window of the Noc Noc, damn near killing me and Kate, right?" I asked.

He nodded smugly. "At the time I didn't know you from the planter, you were just another customer. But I actually knew

Brian, and was real sorry it happened that way. I was after Kate that night—almost got her, too. That would have saved a bunch of lives." Another shrug. "After that I started to get a few second thoughts. If I could have switched sides right then I might have done it—might be better for the world if Kate's the rich bitch, rather than Cee Cee. But there can only be one winner, and there was no way I could change horses in the middle of this shit creek." Steve smoothly jerked his revolver from its holster, twirled it twice and then re-holstered.

I found it very interesting that did not give me a frisson of fear, just a major annoyance. "So who threw Amanda off her balcony?" I gritted out.

"That was Celeste. She needed to know where Kate went and how she was traveling. She snuck in and hid in the closet and heard what you said and watched you bugger her. You perverted turd burglar," he chuckled. "She didn't want the poor little girl to tell anyone else. So she conked you and sent you down the stairs. Then she snuck up on Amanda, who was kind of comatose from your little session, and hit her on the back of the head real hard. That girl is stronger than she looks and she looks pretty strong. She hoped that with a little luck they would figure you for the dirty deed, but you skated out on that one. You know, if you were half as smart as you are lucky, well shit, you'd really be a force to deal with."

He pulled out that fucking gun again and kind of fondled it. "Wild Bill's gun used .36 caliber balls and you had to pack each cylinder separately. The whole wheel could be pulled out. People had belts with spare cylinders. It must have been a real pain in the ass killing people back then, but old James Butler was pretty good at it according to the legend. He was supposed to have killed one guy at seventy five yards with one of these."

He pointed it right between my eyes and cocked it. There was a very big hole at the end of its barrel. "You feel like trying a hundred-yard dash for the grand prize of continuing to breathe?"

I stared into his eyes. He was enjoying our conversation too much to blow me away right now.

"So why kill poor little Kansas down at Diamond Dolls? She didn't really know squat. She just liked the way Kate ate pussy?" I asked, my face probably as red as Rooby's hood.

Steve stared hard at me. I thought I had gotten a little grudging respect from him by not cringing. He slowly lowered the hammer on the cannon and stuck it back in its holster. "You know you ain't getting out of here alive, don't ya? I just can't have you screwing this deal up anymore. Following me out here was a real stupid move for a fairly smart guy. Ah, what the hell, I guess I can answer a few more questions. Cee Cee met her in the ladies' shitter and started talking to her when she saw that silly homemade tattoo she drew on her arm. That thing got her killed. She convinced her that she was a lipstick dyke, which I suppose is at least halfway true, and convinced her she should go upstairs with her for a little quality rug munching. And of course the girl bragged about her latest little lezzy liaison and where Kate had got off to. Celeste didn't know you already had that information. She saw you sitting in the audience and figured she could get a jump ahead of you, freeze you out of the play. I beat feet out to the Mustang and lay in wait for her to get off work. I was real surprised when you showed up to spoil the play. Like I said before, you have been a real pain in the ass. But that's gonna end real soon. Anything else you gotta know before I blow your lunch all over the desert?"

I shifted my feet a little to get some better traction. "How about poor little Sassy and Slim? How the fuck did you know where to find them?"

Steve actually giggled at this one. "You can blame that one on old Walter himself, and some kind of luck. Walter trusted Cee Cee and loved to talk about the old days when Kate was just a little girl. Turns out they used to go down to that spot for a little picnic and some innocent skinny dipping. Walter was an asshole in a lot of ways but he wasn't a pedophile, he just liked swimming and lying naked in the sun. And you know how little kids love to run around naked. There ain't many places you can do that in northern Nevada," he shrugged. "He described the place to Celeste a few times. So that day we split up, two cars and driving 80, trying to find her. Well, it got sort of late and she was about ready to give up and head back to the motel when she recognized that cut-off. She parked and walked in, just to check it out. She saw the car that Kate was driving and a woman lying next to it in a sleeping bag, passed out cold and stinking of rum—thought it was Kate. Cee Cee cut her throat and beat feet out a there. I never said she wasn't just a little out of control. Shit, she's under a lot of pressure and our coke consumption has gone up accordingly."

"Yup, some kind of luck for Slim and Sassy," I mused.

"Anything else you need to know before I shoot your dumb ass and put you in a shallow grave out here in the desert?" His voice had a strange, strained edge that told me I was as close to death right then as I had ever been in my not-uneventful life.

I stared into his squinty eyes as that thought kept running over and over in what passes for my mind.

"There's a lot of shit I'd like to know, but probably nothing else you can tell me," I made my voice as calmly obnoxious as possible. "So pull out your big old dick substitute and do it. If you are waiting for me to start begging for my life, it's gonna be a long day."

Steve pulled the gun out with a leisurely shrug and cocked it as he brought it up to point right at my nose. I was still twenty feet away from him and the urge to charge him with the sword right in front of me was almost overpowering. I didn't do it. I just stared at him trying to look as contemptuous as I could.

He suddenly raised the barrel as he lowered the hammer and turned to the open door of the car to throw the gun on the front seat. Then he pulled out his aluminum baseball bat and turned back toward me. "Fuck you, cocksucker. I think I'll just fucking beat you to death."

I launched myself at him, throwing the scabbard away and whipping the cane-sword over my head like a horse soldier riding down a poor benighted Indian.

He instinctively raised the bat over his head to block the downward thrust. I counted on him doing that and if he hadn't I'd probably be dead, or near dying.

I brought my left hand out of my back pocket flicking my switchblade open just in time to stab him right in the center of his big neck. Blood gushed all over my hand and arm—hot blood. Steve's mouth opened and through the bloody bubbles he said, "Momma!"

■ ■ ■

CHAPTER FIFTEEN

Steve's dying reflex was to raise his large hard knee violently into my crotch as he fell over backward. This launched me over his body as it showered me in his blood.

Killing people is a very messy business. You can write that one down if you want but it might not be the bumper sticker you want on your SUV.

I ended up with a mouth full of sand a couple of feet beyond him. My nose was bleeding, but not nearly as seriously as Steve's neck. I rolled over and turned to face him. One of his legs was still twitching. It stopped after a minute.

The world seemed very still. I pulled my legs up tight against my chest. I felt like a psychopathic cook had been gleefully tenderizing my testicles.

I knew this job was only half done; one wacko down and one to go. But I thought I deserved a few minutes of relaxation, just a little lazy time to roll around in the dirt savoring the agony, while I let the blood on my clothes congeal.

Eventually this got old, and I checked out my ability to walk around, rubbing my balls. I picked up my cane-sword and its scabbard, pulled my knife out of the still-oozing wound in Steve's neck.

I contemplated the gun lying on the front seat, but I had a couple of problems taking it. The more practical one was it was a very unique weapon and there had to be a paper trail leading from it to Steve, and I'd like the trail to end there, not continue on to me. The other was one of the few Buddhist tenets I try to live by, the law of Karma, or what goes around comes around. In other words, I promised myself I would never kill someone for profit. So I left the gun, his wallet and everything else that had anything to do with him and limped on back to my car trunk.

I stripped to the skin and washed off the blood with water from the anti-freeze jug I keep in the trunk. Then I put on clean clothes, everything, even shoes. I really liked my boots, but not enough to have them put me in jail.

I was not sorry that big Steve was dead, considering the only other outcome that could have come from this confrontation. But I'd just as soon not have to prove that it was self-defense to a jury of Nevada residents. So I stuck all the bloody and soiled clothes in a plastic bag and stashed it in the trunk to dispose of later.

I headed back to Elko. Fortunately the highway was empty when I got back onto the main road. I stopped a few miles down the road, dug a hole and buried my bloody clothes. Neatness, after all, is ten percent of your final grade. Then I drove on into town.

I eased past the major hotel casino about eight P.M. and headed for the red-light district. I circled the block where Inez's occupies the corner spot with its proudly garish neon sign advertising the twin activities dancing and diddling.

Behind the club was the black Impala Kate had driven here from Seattle. All four tires had been slashed. I parked half a block away and, stealthily as I could, walked back.

The brothel's front door was ajar and all the lights were on. The entrance opened into a foyer next to a fairly small bar with a dancer pole, six barstools, a puddle of spilled beer on the bar top, and a white male bartender, lying on the floor in a puddle of bloody beer.

I pulled the sword about halfway out of my cane scabbard, as I eased past the dead bartender towards the cribs and party rooms in the back. There was a hallway with a bathroom on one side and a kitchen on the other. No sounds, no music or giggles. No orgasmic moans. Nothing.

The hallway took a right turn and the first door was painted green. A sign over the door said "LET US PARTY ON." That sounded like a good idea, so I turned the handle and eased the door open—sword in one hand and cane barrel in the other.

Red drapes crossed one wall with mirrors on the other three. Red throw rugs on the floor led to a three-step platform with a large bubbling hot tub, surrounded by white tiles.

The place seemed deserted, but the drapes attracted my attention for some reason. Did the drapes move? Sway? I approached them, sword point first, to tickle the place where the curtains came together.

As my blade tip touched the curtain and parted them a fraction of an inch, an aluminum baseball bat shot out from between them in an upward arc from floor level, headed right for my crotch.

I twisted sideways to take a vicious blow on my right knee. The pain all but took my consciousness away as I fell over backwards, ending up flat on my back on the furry red throw rug.

The bat continued up to the ceiling, held by the right hand of a not entirely unexpected apparition. Celeste was dressed in bright red panties, of course, plus a red negligee and a headband with little red horns on it. She looked like a hooker from the depths of hell as she swung the baseball bat in her right hand, with a straight razor open and flashing in her left.

This murderous nut job and her recently deceased boyfriend had hotter fucking bats than the Mariners outfield, and they seemed to want to use my body for the grand slam.

"You silly motherfucker," Celeste screamed. "You're supposed to be history by now. Where's Steve?"

"Deader than disco," I gritted out past the pain.

"Well, good. He was next on my list, after Sister Kate anyway!"

"Were you going to do Steve like you did Walter Hickok?"

"Probably, except I wouldn't have enjoyed it as much." Celeste laughed and raised her bat.

I got ready to roll one way or the other to avoid that shiny baseball bat. Once again I was in a very nasty spot. If I lived through the day, I would really have to think about slowing down on my mayhem quotient.

The door I had come through suddenly slammed open, crashing into the wall, and a vision of violent loveliness charged right into the face of my tormenting tart, screaming, "Get off of him, you skanky cunt!"

Kate Hickok had arrived in the proverbial nick of time, the sexy savior of my personal bacon. She was wearing a robin's-egg blue thong and a matching sports bra and was the most enchanting single vision I had seen in my entire life.

Kate charged, both her arms straight out in front of her like a football lineman pulling an illegal maneuver, slamming both hands into Celeste's scarlet nylon-covered tits, and locked on, hard.

Cee Cee—as the late Steve had called her—yelped like a puppy whose tail had been stepped on. There was a great ripping sound, like a long beer fart, that left most of her negligee in Kate's hands as Cee Cee catapulted backwards into the step that led to the hot tub.

Cee Cee went ankles over ass in a reverse somersault, right into the water with a room-drenching splash.

I got a flash of her large floppy breasts, with nipples the size of beer coasters. Kate leapt in right behind her, still screaming imprecations until she got a big mouthful of hot water. Celeste surfaced on the other side of the tub wiping water out of her eyes.

I tried to get up and join in the fray of the girls-gone-homicidal. Who wouldn't? Especially since my continued existence depended on the outcome. My knee collapsed with a flash of agony and I realized I was going to be an interested spectator in this final round of the tournament. My fate was in Kate's hands, in what had to be a fight literally to the death.

Kate came up on my side of the tub, facing me, briefly rubbing water out of her eyes. Her blue bra was gone and her thong was around her thighs. She, by the way, had small perky tits with nipples the size of thimbles.

I screamed. "Behind you, Goddamnit, behind you!" as Celeste's hands closed around Kate's throat.

Kate's mouth opened wide and round. Tub water shot out all the way to my chest. She brought both arms up over her head to grab handfuls of Celeste's hair. They both screamed loudly.

I noticed Kate's thong slipping down past her knees as she butt-bumped Celeste back to the middle of the tub. She was, after all, a pole dancer and a stripper, and a lot stronger than she looked. Her legs shot up in the air. That soggy blue thong landed next to me as she planted her feet against the edge of the tub and with a mighty thrust, sent them both back across the tub.

Celeste's head cracked hard against the mirror on the back wall with a big old crunch. Her hands fell away from Kate's neck and, with the amazing agility of a gymnast, Kate slid down the bigger girl's body, until her head was between Celeste's legs. It looked like she was trying to appease her with a little pussy-licking.

It was a little late for that, I thought, and Kate obviously thought so, too. She wrapped her arms around Celeste's waist, flipped her long lovely legs toward the ceiling to wrap her thighs around Celeste's neck, her ass crack against Celeste's chin, propelling Celeste's head toward the center of the pool. They looked for a moment like a pair of tumble bugs.

Then Kate was standing up, her arms squeezing Celeste's waist in an extreme bear hug as she bit Celeste's crotch as hard as she could, shaking her head like a terrier with a big rat. Blood flew from the sides of her mouth. Celeste's legs wind-milled and gyrated, her head and shoulders under the water.

That seemed to go on forever, or maybe it was only minutes. I really couldn't tell you which, but finally Celeste stopped moving. Bubbles stopped coming up out of the water. There was a great belching sound and the smell of human shit wafted over me.

Kate finally let go of Celeste's waist in disgust and Celeste splashed down into the hot water. Kate stood naked in the hot tub. The water came to her upper thighs which were parted, still clenched around Celeste's neck.

"You ain't gonna kill anybody else's daddy, Bitch!" Kate gritted through clenched teeth.

Celeste floated a few inches beneath the water with just her scratched and bloody nipples above the surface. She was still wearing the red panties she had been so proud of. They clung to her like a transparent scarlet membrane, with her dark thatch of pubic hair standing starkly out from the surrounding skin. Her bowels had loosened in death, turning the water a cloudy brown between her legs.

I half-crawled, half-dragged myself across the tile floor to sprawl beside the pool on the garish pink-tiled lip. My right knee was way beyond throbbing into some other upper realm of pain and had already swollen enough to stretch my dirty Levis tight.

Kate stood there for quite a while, staring straight ahead with her cobalt-blue eyes very wide and unblinking. A pink and brown statue with shoulder freckles and a tattoo streaked with scratches and blood.

Finally Kate pushed down on Celeste's chest, un-straddled her, and crawled slowly out of the other side of the tub. Her badly bitten buttocks were bloody and already turning black and blue. She turned on the shower in the wall beside the tub, picked up a bottle of body wash and poured it over her head and body, rubbing herself vigorously, washing away the remnants of the hot tub. Once finished, she grabbed a towel and came over to my side of the hot tub.

Kate stood over me as she rubbed herself dry. Finished with her drying, Kate reached down and grabbed me by the pony tail. It was a gentle grab, but it got my attention. She already had that, of course. I hadn't taken my eyes off her for half an hour or so.

"You know what your problem is, Angus, my dear?" She wagged my head back and forth. "You are pussy-whipped." She grabbed her crotch and rubbed it. "Oh, not my pussy, just pretty girl pussy in general. And it is going to get you in a lot trouble for as long as you live."

I nodded. This sounded reasonable.

"I knew about Celeste—well, maybe that's not quite accurate. I knew someone was sniffing around my life and my ass. I didn't know what a homicidal bitch she would turn out to be, but I knew I was going to be in danger when Grandma died, or even got sick. When the shit hit the fan at the Noc Noc, I knew I had to get out of town fast. I hoped if I left that card on my bed with Amanda's picture, my dad would hire you to follow me—I knew I was going to need some help. I swear I didn't know Amanda was in danger, or that so many people were going to die, especially my dad." Tears welled up in her eyes.

She let go of my head and dropped the damp towel on it. I watched her walk over to grab a terrycloth robe hanging on a wall hook.

She put it on as she talked. "I thought that one of us would end up dead and I didn't want it to be me. But I didn't want to lose her altogether before it came to some kind of conclusion. I sure as hell didn't want to be looking over my shoulder for the rest of my life. That's why I didn't just take off for Mexico and get myself lost."

She shook her hair out, slipped her feet into some handy flip flops and came back to where I was lying. She bent over and stuck her hand in my pocket, taking out my car keys. "That bitch really fucked up my ride—too bad, too, because it was a sweet ride. I'll have to get it fixed for Amanda's fisherman. It's the least I could do. And now, with Daddy dead, I'm pretty rich." Poor Amanda's fisherman boyfriend would have had another reason to be sad if Celeste had won.

Kate continued, "Actually, you are gonna get it fixed after you get yourself fixed up. I'll send you some money, and give you a lot more when you drive it back to Seattle. You won't have to get involved with any more crazy bitches for quite a while if you don't want to—but of course, being you, you'll want to. I'm also going to send you a crackerjack lawyer my daddy used a lot. He'll get you out of trouble with the law. Daddy said this guy could get a charge of sodomy reduced to following too close. So, Steve is dead, too?"

I nodded. "Oh, yeah. Steve is real dead."

Kate nodded and looked sad for a moment. "I always thought he had a kind of crush on me." Then she gave me her big smile and even laughed a little.

This lady recovers like a fencing foil.

"Now I'm gonna leave you here to deal with the cops; I don't really have the patience for it, besides I need to get away from this place, so I can grieve and put all this behind me.   All I ask is about a ten-minute head start and then call the cops.   In the morning you will be contacted by Michael Danko and as many of my daddy's other lawyers as you need. And believe me, Daddy has—or had—a bunch of lawyers."

Kate bent down to give me a kiss on the cheek.   Her robe fell open, showing me the scratches and gouges on her tits and belly again.

"You better get some Neosporin on those bites and scratches, kiddo.   That witch was poison," I said.

She gave me another smile and she was out the door.

■ ■ ■

CHAPTER SIXTEEN

I heard the familiar throaty growl of Rooby starting up and a spit of gravel as Kate drove off, headed for the highway.

I figured I'd give her twenty minutes and then crawl out to the bar and find a phone. As it turned out I didn't even have to move.

A small sound from the hallway reached my ears. It gave me a start. I'd thought there were only two members of the Celeste cartel and they were both dead. One, slowly revolving in the hot tub, a little below the surface and soiling the bubbling hot water; the other attracting the gustatory curiosity of the little desert birds and critters. So I should have had no more enemies in northern Nevada, unless you count the entire law enforcement community that I was about to have an intense adversarial relationship with.

But life had been throwing a lot of surprises at me lately, so I was pleasantly amazed when a petite oriental girl in a black thong and matching lace bra timidly came into the room.

That's right: I was in the fun room of a whorehouse. Duh!

Her pretty dark eyes got very large when she saw what was floating in the hot tub and her nose started twitching like a bunny rabbit when she smelled Celeste's dying shit.

"Shit!" she said succinctly.

"Exactly," I heartily answered. "And death! Where were you hiding?"

"In the big party room in the back. Salome came busting back there, told all us girls to get in the big room and get something to hit with. And stay there 'til she came to get us. We did it, too. Everybody likes Salome."

"Not everybody." I tried a little wry humor but it came out kind of plaintive due to the amount of pain my knee was causing me. "You might want to call 911. Salome probably won't be around for awhile, but you won't be lonely. Every cop in the county is about to descend on Inez's Dancing and Diddling and they probably won't dance or diddle but they are gonna ask you a whole bunch of questions. Just answer them as best you can."

There was a great groan from the bar as the bartender regained consciousness. That was a good sign, I guessed. Although I'd bet he was going to be a little cranky.

I heard a baritone voice growl, "Fuck!"

I was right.

Two more girls were peeking at me from the doorway—both pretty young oriental ladies. One in sweat pants and a T-shirt that says, "Kiss Me I'm Irish." For some reason I found this very funny and started laughing like a loon on LSD. It could have been the fact that I had lived through this little adventure. But more likely I was just plain losing it. It should make an interesting defense.

All the girls left me alone in a hurry. I heard a jumble of raised voices coming from the bar, then the baritone started talking to the 911 operator. My life was about to become complicated and tedious in equal proportions.

It was going to be a very long day, because I was going to lawyer up. Big time.

Now, if you have been paying attention, I'm sure you have realized what a great deal of respect I have for the law enforcement community and the deep affection they have in return for me. Yup. So I hope you will not think I'm being sarcastic when I ask if you have ever watched five monkeys try to fuck a football. That's kind of what I witnessed over the next five hours as my prediction turned out to be incredibly prescient.

The Elko City Police arrived in force and started bumping into each other and dithering. I couldn't really blame them. It was a wet and juicy scene. A dead woman in the hot tub leaking shit, a highly disreputable-looking customer on the floor reclining while he watched his knee swell up to the size of that self-same football I mentioned before. A small gaggle—I'm not sure what you call a bunch of hookers but I'd call them a "grope" of girls—looking fetchingly bewildered. We had it all.

Eventually I ended up at the Elko County Hospital getting my leg splinted and then in a private room with my very own door guard. I failed to answer questions for several hours.

"My lawyer will be here in the morning," I kept saying, almost like I believed it. But for some reason it didn't stop the various public servants from getting their panties all in a wad.

My doctor was a thirty-something woman with a white lab coat and nice neat proportions who looked at me somewhat askance.

In all fairness, which you know I always try for, I couldn't really blame her, what with the squinty-eyed plainclothes cops standing around fondling the bulges under their arms and looking at me like I was the guy that taught Hannibal Lecter his table manners. I tried a little flirting, just because I couldn't help myself, but my doctor briskly ignored me. She refused my request for an anal thermometer with a wrinkled-nose sniff, which was all it deserved, and basically let them badger me for quite a while.

Finally she relented enough to firmly shoo everyone out of the room and shot something in my ass—not in a good way—and I went out like a defective string of Christmas lights.

I woke up about four in the afternoon, feeling just a little less like homemade shit than I had when I went to sleep.

My mouth tasted like it had recently been the scene of a love-in for a dozen gerbils.

I located the push button for room service and tried for a nurse with something liquid I could stick in my mouth. She arrived promptly, already holding a glass of something that looked a lot like Tang. Well, a frosty PBR was not a real possibility. I know my limitations.

She handed it to me with a look that would curdle my breast milk, if indeed I had any.

I quaffed it in a single gulp while she watched and practiced her lip curl. I was not going to make a lifelong friend out of her, it would seem. She grunted and stalked out with her chubby buttocks rigid.

There was a man sitting very quietly in the corner, staring at me like I was going to suddenly jump out of bed and run from the room. There might be something farther from the truth, but I couldn't think what it would be at the moment.

He looked like a kind of a low-rent Tommy Lee Jones in a sharp charcoal grey suit and an expression that gave me a clue where the gerbils went after leaving my mouth.

It started to come back to me as my consciousness slowly returned. This guy was the police chief of Elko. Why, was I not thrilled? I couldn't remember his name for what was left of the life of me, but he was very generous with the ration of shit he had given me a few hours ago. He got slowly to his feet and sauntered over. His coat slid open to show off his low slung-gun belt and pearl-handled pistol. I think the next time I come to Nevada I'm going to bring a howitzer.

"Hi, Chief. I'm touched you sat here and worried about my health." My mouth was still sometimes not my best ally.

The Chief looked irritated but almost a trifle subdued and I didn't know why.

"Listen, scumbag," he said pleasantly, "my name is Sheriff Buck Shepard and if I really need any of your shit, I'll just jump up and down on your head 'til I get as much as I want."

He kind of smiled, and I kind of believed him. I wasn't in Seattle any more.

"Now, I'm about to usher a lady in here who is very important to me and this city. So if you value the use of the one good leg you've got left, I'd treat her like the gentleman you never were. Am I getting through your thick ugly head?" he asked with a look of serious menace that got through even to me.

I nodded. Not much point in getting in a pissing match when you are laying flat on your back.

He turned and stalked from the room abruptly and stopped just outside the door, holding it open as a very old woman slowly entered. The Sheriff seemed ready to take her arm and assist her to a chair but she dismissed his attentions with a slight, imperious wave of her left hand. He closed the door as she eventually made her way to the chair beside the bed and lowered herself into it as gingerly as if her ass was priceless Ming China.

I thought I could guess who she was, and her ass was probably worth more than the most expensive tea cup.

We looked at each other for a while.

Did you ever see a great, very quirky movie named "Harold and Maude"? I love that film. The lady who plays Maude was Ruth Gordon. She had a long and successful career, including several movies with Clint Eastwood, among other things. Well, this lady looked a little like her on a bad day, a very bad day, after six months on a way too stringent diet.

I don't have much expertise in the realm of woman's fashion, but her tailored tan suit and white blouse just bespoke a kind of class and money my whole wardrobe would never get close to. Not that it wanted to.

"I am Emma Boulette," she said in a very wispy voice, "and I'm dying."

There was not a trace of self-pity in her voice.

I nodded. "Angus Vieira, ma'am."

"I know your name and I know quite a lot about you. And, if I've figured it out right you might have done me a great service," she said, and her lips quirked in a way that reminded me of one of Kate's expressions. You could tell she had been a very beautiful woman back when giants walked the earth.

I nodded and shrugged just slightly, because pretty much everything still hurt. "I did a job for Kate's father, for which I was paid pretty well. If I helped Kate stay alive that gave me great pleasure, but it wasn't entirely an altruistic trip," I said modestly.

Her mouth twisted into a wry smile. "I've had thousands of girls work for me over the years. Some of them took a great deal of pleasure in their work, but they didn't give it away very often. I tended to discourage that." She sounded a little stronger as the conversation progressed. "But if I was fifty years younger, I might just do you for free. Sort of take one for the team." She followed that declaration with a very dry chuckle that turned into a small coughing fit.

"Well, I'm a day or so away from my full amatory capabilities, so I'll give you a while to change your mind," I could still manage a wink and leer.

She smiled again. "You talk funny even when you're blowing smoke up my ass."

Then she looked serious again. "I hear that Kate's dad is dead? And so is the person who killed him?"

I nodded. Surrounded by cops I was not going to say anything that could end up in a court of law. She seemed to understand this well because she said, "You've got some friends in your corner of the ring that are not without influence."

She was being rather modest there I'd say.

"Walter was a screaming asshole in many ways. But he wasn't that bad a father. That was a bad way to die. He deserved a better end."

My thoughts exactly. Again I just nodded.

She gave me a small smile. "I'll let you get some rest. You've been a very busy boy."

She slowly rose to her feet and Sheriff Buck opened the door and took her arm with great deference. I was right in my hunch that the room was bugged. He slowly ushered her out.

He gave me a look that seemed to have a lot less venom and contempt than his former attitude. Once she had gone he came back in the room and looked at me in thoughtful silence for a few minutes.

I looked back in drowsy pain.

He left and no one came in to take his place in the corner chair. I guessed they had finally figured out I was not much of a flight risk. I took a nap in the hospital silence, only to awaken when a young woman in a candy striper's pink dress and white blouse came into the room. It was getting dark so I had probably slept for a couple of hours.

She was pushing one of those hospital carts and came over to my bed with a small smile on her face. She pulled a container that looked like a gravy boat with a cover and a long spout out of the cart, gave me a tiny grin and blushed as she asked, "Do you have to make pee-pee, by any chance?"

She had coppery colored hair and freckles that became more apparent because of the blush.

Before even I could come up with a witty bit of repartee, she had my covers down and my gown up. She gently put my cock in the opening of the gravy boat.

Now on an ordinary day, or what passes for an ordinary day in my life these days, her just touching my fun gun would likely make it start to swell up, making it difficult to take a leak, but truth to tell, I had to piss like the proverbial fast horse. I gratefully filled her jar. She took it into the bathroom and flushed it away, coming back into the room with a damp washcloth that she used to gently clean my cock and balls.

So far I hadn't said a word, which was strangely unlike me. Maybe I really was sick, or delirious.

"I'm gonna give you about an hour and a half to stop doing that," I finally managed to say, with what I hoped was a teacher-like smile.

She grinned back. "Do you want to know a secret?" she asked, making her blue eyes big and round.

I nodded eagerly.

She put her finger to her lips in a time-honored shush and bent over to whisper in my ear. "I'm not wearing any underpants," she breathed in my ear.

Yup. There was a noticeable sudden swelling as she danced around the middle of the room with her skirt up around her waist. Not a single hair on her pretty little pussy or round freckled ass.

She continued her dance, to my intense pleasure. Then she was back to fasten her mouth on my erection. I was so hard by now that a cat couldn't scratch it.

I have had quite a few great blow jobs in my life. It's one of my favorite forms of entertainment. Seldom had anyone done it better than she did it over the next half an hour or so—bringing me within a single contraction of coming lots of times before she actually let me do it.

She kept her mouth fastened to my cock for what seemed like a long time after I was through spasming and squirting. Then she slowly straightened up with a tight-lipped smile.

I have long had a theory about the Mona Lisa: I think she couldn't quite decide whether she should swallow it or spit it out. My little candy striper decided in seconds with an audible gulp. Then she winked at me and said, "Emma Boulette sends her thanks." She wheeled her cart around and flashed me a final over-the-shoulder smile.

■ ■ ■

CHAPTER SEVENTEEN

I woke up after sleeping long and hard. The clock said twelve and it was light outside, which told me it was the next day. My stomach told me it was noon. I have no idea how much local juice it took to keep nurses and doctors from awakening a hapless patient every four hours to take a sleeping pill or take a thermometer up the ass, but I'm sure it was considerable. I naturally had to piss like the large animal of your choice. I didn't think my little candy striper cocksucker was going to be back any time soon, so I disconnected my foot harness and mentally prepared for the arduous journey to the urinal. It wasn't until I actually got ready for the six-inch leap to the floor that I noticed the guy sitting in the corner.

Tall and whippet-thin—probably well over sixty but healthy and strong, he was wearing a dark-grey, designer suit worth at least a couple of grand, with a pin-striped off-white shirt and burgundy tie that alone probably cost as much as all the clothes I had parked on the shelf in the corner of the room. He was giving me a thin-lipped smile that seemed to actually contain a degree of amicable good humor. He stared at me silently for a couple of moments, as I sat frozen on the side of the hospital bed. I was gonna take a wild guess that this was my lawyer and new best friend.

"Why don't you go ahead and take a leak. Then we'll have a conversation," he said in a soothing tenor.

I nodded and took the great leap to the floor. Surprisingly my knee didn't buckle or give me more than a twinge of grief.

I slowly made my way to the bathroom without trying to close the open back of my cutesy gown and did not bother to close the door as I took one of the most satisfying pisses of my life. Shyness and modesty were never part of my collection of character flaws.

He came to sit on the chair beside the bed and continued to stare at me like I was a fairly amusing phony antique vase.

I stared back like I thought he might purchase me and give me to someone who would not know I was worthless.

Finally he spoke.

"My name is Michael Danko and I am your lawyer—if that's all right with you."

He paused and I nodded encouragingly. "I probably need all the help I can get," I said.

He shook his head and chuckled. "You might not be in as much trouble as you think you are and probably richly deserve to be," he said convolutedly.

This interested me immediately because I'd been having some rather disturbing group shower dreams.

He continued. "Either through some kind of dumb luck, which is my personal best guess, or some kind of heroic plan, which I feel is highly unlikely, you have some very influential and rich people who suddenly wish you well and trouble free—at least for the moment."

He talked like a lawyer but I could listen to that all afternoon.

He continued. "The black Impala is a sweet ride. It's out in the parking lot. Take care of it and get it back to Seattle in the same shape it's in." He reached into his pocket to hand me a set of keys on a brand new key chain that said, "Souvenir of Las Vegas." It was real sharp.

"It's got five brand-new top of the line tires, a tune up and an oil change it badly needed. I guess the person who drove it down here was in kind of a hurry," he almost smiled. "The tank is full of gas and if I were *you*, or anyone remotely like you, I would put my clothes on, and get the fuck out of this town while you've still got a 'stay out of jail and be free' card. It could expire at any moment." This time he did smile. "Tell a certain mutual friend she'll be getting a big bill."

There are some things you don't have to tell me twice. I was out of bed and peeling off my drafty gown even as he turned to leave the room, which he did without a backward glance.

I found a side entrance and headed for the parking lot at a fast limp.

Right in front of the hospital, the newly washed black Impala convertible sat in its muscular loveliness. That was the good news. The bad news was leaning up against the front fender.

Sheriff Buck Shepard looked casual and menacing in almost equal proportions—

perhaps a little more menacing. I wondered if maybe my "stay out of jail card" expired while I was pulling on my pants.

He had obviously seen me, so I soldiered on up to stand in front of him. I was in no shape to outrun anybody, even if I had someplace to go.

I stopped about four feet in front of him and we stared at each other. When and if I got out of that town, I wanted to go a long time without any confrontations at all. Yeah, right.

Sheriff Shepard opened his coat so he could fondle his six-shooter while he gave me the look of steely resolve and disdain that I had grown incredibly tired of staring back at, and finally broke the silence. "You make my handcuffs itch! I really long for the good-old-days when we had a special room way under the jail, all nicely padded, just for entertaining your brand of troublemaker. But this time I'm just gonna watch you get in that fancy muscle car, that you don't even deserve to be thrown under, and get the fuck out of my town, my county—hell, even my state. But before you go, I'm gonna make you a single promise. If I ever see your ugly head in Elko again, I'm going to throw you in a dark cell with the biggest, nastiest, meanest Sodomite I can find in my whole penal system. Now get the fuck out of here."

He turned his back on me and started to saunter across the parking lot.

I don't often thank God for something, so let's just say I was really glad that the Impala started up on the first try.

I rolled in to Carlin, Nevada, about an hour and a half later and took the small highway down to Sharon's Brothel. Sharon was standing in the doorway just the way she was the last time I saw her. That seemed like a long time ago, now; time gets a little funny when you are fighting for your life.

Sharon gave me a big wave and grin as I parked and headed to the door at a reasonably casual limp.

"How come every time you show up or leave, you look kind of worse for the wear?" she asked with a soft chuckle.

"I think this time is going to be a little different. I hope so anyway—unless maybe, Tricksy smothers me with those fine buttocks of hers." Ah, I had my lecherous grin back. I thought I was well on the road to recovery.

Sharon moved aside and ushered me onto a bar stool... back in my favorite saddle, again. Well, second favorite anyway. She popped the top on a "Heinie" and slid it my way.

"This one's on the house 'cause I'm glad to see you crawled out the other end of that situation you were dealing with, more or less intact. Is it over? Is that pretty girl gonna come back here and work for me? What happened to the ogre with the Babe Ruth swing?" Sharon seemed to have been thinking about me.

"That's probably as good a way of putting it as any. No, I'd say the pretty girl came into enough money that for a long time she can be real selective who she's with when she sheds her panties. And let's just say the big fella got dropped from the team. How's Tricksy and Charlie and life on the back roads of Carlin?"

I finished that beer in about five swallows and started on the next one.

"Thirsty lad, aren't we?" Sharon said with admiration. "Well, I'm a girl short for a while. You remember those truckers that rolled in just as you were leaving, Driver Dan and his buddy, Bob Bailey? Well, they stayed about a day, seems they were dead-heading back to the coast and felt like a little R and R. They spent some money, and I 'comped' them some, too—couple of good old boys. Then about noon of the next day, Dan, with kind of a sheepish grin on his face, rolls into the bar arm and arm with Tricksy. Seems like they hit it off really well, and she's decided to give up this budding career and start truck driving with him and Bob. Bob ain't quite the player Dan is, so he was sleeping in the truck. It's going to be real cozy in that sleeper for a while." She shrugged. "I wish her nothing but the best. The sporting life, as Hemingway called it in 'To Have and Have Not,' is always here if it doesn't work out for her. I got a box of her working lingerie and her Bettie Page picture back in the storage shed. But I got a little Spanish chili pepper out back that could spice up your afternoon. What do you think? Want to meet her?"

I gave a regretful shake of the head.

"I love the brown ladies. I'm kind of an equal opportunity horndog, but let's just say that not everyone back in Elko is a big fan of me and mine, so I think I'd better put a bunch more miles between me and him."

Sharon nodded like she might know a bit more about what I was talking about than she had told me. Well, it was a tight community.

"Okay, one more beer. No charge for these, but you have to promise you'll pass this way again and spend some time and money... and bodily fluids."

I gave her a pinky promise.

I got back on Highway 80 west and a couple of hours later blew right through Battle Mountain, past the cutoff to Donna's Brothel. I didn't have to look for Kate any more. I might have been getting a little burned out on whorehouses. I didn't think that would last very long. I sure hoped not. I'm much too young to become an adult and give up my monumental struggle with puberty.

I hit Winnemucca about midnight and headed for the same motel where I last saw Walter Hickok alive. I got a room just three doors down from the room where old Walter and I had our last chat. I threw my bag on the bed and, with a wry mental shrug to his memory, turned on the television to the same boring soft porn channel.

If I ever reach the unlikely situation where I find that I need a secretary, I'm going to give her a real thorough background check. But right then, I just needed a good night's sleep. I flopped down on the bed and fell asleep to what might have been the same pneumatic young blonde, faking the same orgasm as the last time I had that station on.

I got an almost unprecedented ten hours of dreamless sleep and woke up around ten in the morning. There's something to be said for a mundane existence where no one is trying to kill you and you, for your part, are not trying to keep someone from getting killed.

I headed across the street to a casino and dug into an enormous steak-and-egg breakfast.

On the way back to the motel, I looked down the main drag toward Baud Street, thinking about the story Slim told me in the Wild West Saloon. Sapphire might have been waking up, scratching her lovely brown ass and getting ready to make some guy a very happy boy. My own happy boy tried to urge me to go and see her but the thought of the Sassy and Slim saga sent me back to the motel to check out and head up the highway southwest, through the moonlike desert landscape, toward Reno.

At ten o'clock that night, I drove back down Fourth Avenue to the same crack-head palace I'd stayed in that memorable day I ended up with Kansas/Sarah's blood on my shirt. I needed to go back to Diamond Dolls to tell the manager that her death had been—well, I guess the word I would use is "avenged."

Anyway, he'd done me a big favor by letting me get out of there before the cops arrived, but that could wait until the morning.

The same thin, weary-looking man rented me the same room. He was looking even thinner and wearier. He recognized me with some relief, probably thinking this was one rental where he wouldn't have to evict the tenant at four in the morning with baseball bat in hand.

"Back in town, hey?" he asked rhetorically. "Did you find that girl my wife said you were looking for? I never saw that picture, but she told me about it. I might have been able to help. I got a pretty fair interest in the dancers."

I nodded. "Yup, that's all miles under the wheels now. I just need a place to sleep for the night and I'll be heading northwest."

He looked out in the parking lot at the car I was driving and looked a little puzzled. He almost said something, but then gave me a mental shrug along with a couple of towels and the room key. This was a guy who knew how to mind his own business. That's a sane—and maybe life-saving—trait, if you were going to manage that motel.

I slept well for a few hours, only to be awakened about four-thirty by a very high screeching voice, screaming imprecations. I was almost impressed. It's not everyone who can use "motherfucker" four times in the same sentence. It was coming from the parking lot. My room did not have a window on that wall, so if I wanted to see what was happening I was going to have to open the door. Oh well, my curiosity hadn't gotten me in trouble for a couple of days. I pulled on a pair of shorts and threw the door open.

There was a very pale woman standing in the middle of the parking lot. She was completely naked—not even any shoes. She was, I believe, the skinniest human being I have ever seen in the flesh. She was slowly turning around in a circle with her head thrown back, complaining at the top of her vocal range to the gods or the stars or her imaginary demons. Her long black hair had not been washed in a month, at a guess. Absolutely white skin, like she had been living in the bowels of the sewer. Every rib and spinal bone had its own shadow in the glare of the pitiless anti-theft lights that shone down from the roof. Thick patches of hair sprouted from her armpits and from a couple of inches below her "outie" belly button to where her legs joined at her crotch.

She turned her back to me and suddenly bent over to pick something up. From the back, she looked like a two-by-four with a mossy knothole near one end. As she stood back up with her arm thrown back to hurl the rock at the motel office, she was hit by another beam of light from the arriving police cruiser. Two beefy members of Reno's finest slowly climbed out of the cruiser and approached They seemed to be well-acquainted with her.

The manager, leaning on his baseball bat, watched from the doorway of the office. I watched from the door of my room as the cops handcuffed her and gingerly loaded her in the back of the cruiser and drove off. I waved at the manager, he waved back and I closed the door, shucked my shorts and headed back to bed. There were many stories in the Biggest Little City in the World. I was asleep in ten minutes.

. . .

Diamond Dolls opened at eleven o'clock in the morning, but that was way too early for me to need beer and nearly-naked women. Okay, maybe that's not exactly true. Let's say it's the time of day to drink your own beer and go with amateur naked women. So I walk back up the street to the same small casino for a big breakfast that I went to on my last visit here. Again, I got the feeling that it had been a long time since that occasion but it was really only a few days. I had to keep telling myself that.

Around one in the afternoon, with a huge quantity of steak and scrambled eggs washed down by old Bloody Mary, I walked back to the motel, checked out and drove around the block to park right in front of Diamond Dolls and went in.

I took a seat right in front of the stage and the same curly black-haired waitress was sitting on my lap almost before my butt hit the chair. Her ass wiggled in a very friendly way. It pays to be a big tipper.

"Hi there, traveler." She ran her fingers over my hair and behind my ears. I happily noticed that her skirt hadn't gotten any longer, only today her tiny crotch cover was bright red, which sent a small frisson up my back as I remembered the last time I saw some red panties.

"Hi there yourself, Sugar-Pants." I gave her a hug and copped an almost accidental feel.

She gave my lap a final—well, I hoped not really final—butt rub and sashayed off to get me some beer and one-dollar bills. When she returned, I asked her if Butch was working. She nodded a yes and said she'd tell him I was looking for him when she got a chance. While I waited, I made excellent use of my time, biting dollar bills from and rubbing dollar bills on various panty crotches and cleavages. The Devil, as I have said many times, makes mischief for idle hands. A saying solemnly intoned to me many times by my beloved Mormon Grandma Kate—the first of several Kates to have a profound influence in my life.

Butch came by and sat down beside me, just as my supply of beer and dollar bills became depleted.

"Did you get that sorry bastard?" he asked through gritted teeth. Butch obviously still didn't like people that killed his dancers. Can't say as I blamed him.

"It was more of a bastardess, you might say. And yes, she got 'got' and died in a very undignified manner."

He nodded, somewhat satisfied.

"Anything you want here this afternoon is on the house from this moment on. Beer, lap dances—hell, I'll get one of the girls to blow you in my office if you like," he said.

I thought about it for a couple of minutes as he stared at me and then I regretfully shook my head. "Thanks, and maybe the next time I blow through town I'll take you up on that, if the offer is still open. But today this place still holds to much recent history." Maybe I was getting soft, and not in an untumescent way—If that's a word.

"It will stand as long as I'm here, and since I own part of this joint I don't plan on going anywhere. What better job and work environment could I possibly find? Thanks for stopping by to tell me. I'll call her baby's father and let him know."

We stood up and shook hands. I glanced up at the ceiling a little way over from where I was sitting. The bloodstain was still visible. Butch followed my gaze and shrugged.

"I think of it as kind of a memorial," he said.

I didn't know what to say to that, so I just nodded.

I walked out the door with a wave to my favorite waitress, got in the Impala and headed west on Highway 80.

There just ain't any easy way to head northwest from Reno over to I-5. You have to take a bunch of small two-lane roads through rural California. A lot of it was pretty countryside and I wasn't in that big a hurry, so I kept the Impala at 55 MPH. I'd be very happy if I didn't have to interact with any more policemen of any uniform style, city or state for the foreseeable future. I can dream, can't I?

The top was down, a cold beer in a rubber panty snuggled between my legs and a Warren Zevon tape blared from my cheap cassette player.   Sunshine and seventy degrees.   I had lived through some pretty hairy situations in the last couple of weeks and there was a bunch of money in my back account. Life was real good at the moment.

All that changed in a heartbeat.

I was cruising up a two-lane road about fifty miles east of I-5, coming around a gentle curve with a eighteen-wheeler coming at me in his lane, doing the speed limit, when a small blue piece of shit Toyota Tercel darted out from behind the truck on the curve. The driver (there's a name for this kind of driver: he's called a pass-hole) was going too fast to get back behind the truck but not fast enough to get in front of the truck back in his lane. To my right the road shoulder sloped away at a fairly steep angle, steep enough to roll the Impala if I tried to pull off the road. All I could do was drive straight ahead with my teeth clenched as I visualized dying in a flaming inferno in about fifty feet and five seconds, along with an impatient dickhead who didn't deserve the honor of joining me in my death pyre. Just then, he jerked the wheel to the left and drove off the road and down the incline.

For a minute I thought I had shit my pants, but then I realize my asshole had slammed shut so tight I probably wouldn't shit for a week. All of what happened once again proved, if I needed the lesson, that you don't have any kind of lock on today, let alone tomorrow.

During my fairly long and interesting life, I have come close to the old green ripper on several occasions, so my fear of death per se had kind of atrophied.

My major emotions in the brief moments when I was pretty sure I was going to die that afternoon were regret that it was going to be over for good and all, and a burning desire to choke the living shit out of the oozing prick in the blue Tercel.

I drove on to a motel complex off I-5 just south of Weed and checked in. It was a little fancier than my average rented hovel. There was a balcony outside my room with a spectacular view of Mount Shasta instead of a parking lot full of old cars and crack dealers. I felt that a small celebration was in order.

Dinner was a big steak and baked potato with an over-priced bottle of Merlot.

Sleep came early with no more troubled dreams than usual.

■ ■ ■

CHAPTER EIGHTEEN

I woke up at eight the next morning. A very odd occurrence for me, when I was either retired or just fucking off (I haven't decided which category I fit into—I might need my own category). Another big breakfast and I hit the road ready to fuck, fight or run a foot race. Or at least drive to Oregon—up through the Siskiyous, over Grants Pass and down to Medford by afternoon.

The strip joint in Medford called The Office was still closed. So without that tempting distraction, I pushed on and got into Portland in the early evening.

I pulled into the motel across the street from Union Jack's and checked in, checking my mental and physical well-being as well. Yup, I was at least a quart low on PBR and nude women. So I put my bag in the room and headed for the big UJ.

Big Jim Dunn, the manager and my long-time brother from the Brotherhood of the Sea, was holding down a corner of the bar with a bottle of PBR and his large and imposing elbows.

I got a very firm handshake from a very large hand, a potentially crippling slap on the back and my first bottle of beer on the house. All in all, a damn fine deal.

He noticed my limp as I gimped up onto a barstool.

"You look like you've lived through some interesting times recently. How does the other guy look?" he asked.

I shrugged. "Some good people have died since I saw you last. Some bad people are dead, too. 'So it goes,' as old K. Vonnegut once said." I asked, "Is Bridget still around? I could use another one of her stories." Actually, I could use more from her than a story.

He shook his head. "Nope, she headed back up to your fair Emerald City. I hope she's okay. She might have jumped off the wagon. But we got a lot of pretty, and pretty strange, ladies around here today. Got ten girls working, including one that just moved back up here from eastern Nevada. Her name's Angie." Just then a tall redhead came up and slipped her arms around me from behind, rubbing an impressive pair of knockers on my back.

"Matter of fact those are her boobs you are getting acquainted with even as we speak." She rubbed harder and faster.

"Whom do we have here, Jimmypoo?" she asked, breathing close enough to my ear to get my nipples hard.

"This is my old seagoing amigo, Angus," Dunn said. "Treat him nice and tell him dirty stories and he'll probably go for a couple of your hot private dances. He's got more money than sense."

I laughed. It's hard to deny the truth. I knew I was not driving anywhere that night, not even to another one of Portland's excellent strip joints. Portland was one of the last places in America where you could have a steak dinner with a naked woman's ass inches from your face, a hard drink or a real beer in your hand, and a smoke in the ashtray. But the smoke in the ashtray was not long for this world: they were putting in a No Smoking ordinance at the end of the year. Humans just don't know how to deal with paradise. They always fuck it up somehow.

Jim bought me some drinks and I bought some back. Angie got to drink right along with us, so around midnight, lips had loosened—and I'm not talking about the ones she keeps in her underpants. So I took her into an alcove for a private dance or two, with the stipulation that she'd tell me some kind of kinky story while she looked down on my face, framed by her small, well trimmed, reddish-blonde patch of pubic hair.

"Well, this is just between us, and you will not tell anyone else in Portland this ever. Right?"

I smiled and nodded, which put my nose right in her vaginal cleft. Not a bad place for it.

"I just moved here from Ely, Nevada. You might call it the early stages of sex worker burnout. I was a working girl at the Greenlight, a cathouse at the south end of town. Ever been there?"

I nodded. "You would have trouble finding a brothel in Nevada I haven't been to."

She didn't look unduly impressed.

"So these two guys come in there one night and take me and a young Filipina girl back into the big party room. They spend a lot of money to get us for the whole afternoon and we think it is gonna be a good day, money-wise and just maybe, from a pure sex aspect. They're a couple of young, good-looking boys and we both thought we might just get some happy endings ourselves. That happens sometimes, not all that often in my case. Anyway, what we ended up doing is licking each other's pussy while the two fags fucked each other up the asshole. Now, I'm obviously not a prude, or easily shocked, but I just decided I didn't need anymore of that shit for awhile." She shrugged. "I might end up going back to the business, but for now I'm just shaking my ass and showing my pussy."

"And a lovelier cooze man has seldom seen," I said gallantly as I stuck my lips out in a kissing motion.

She backed away a small distance. "No touching honey. Not in this place or you'll get me canned."

I nodded regretfully. More drinks ensued and by the time I finally staggered back to my room at closing time, I was very horny and much too drunk to do anything about it, even if I'd had an offer.

I fell into deep inebriated sleep as soon as I took my shoes off and had one of the most vivid and strangest dreams I've had since my last acid trip.

It started out in black and white with a very young Elvis Presley standing on a stage singing, "Warden threw a party in the County Jail / Prison band was there / They began to wail / Number forty-seven said to number three / You're the cutest jailbird I ever did see / I sure would be delighted with you bomping me / Come on and do the Jailhouse Rock with me / Let's rock / Everybody let's rock / Everybody in the whole cell block / Was dancing to the Jailhouse Rock."

The song went on and on, and I thought I had never realized before how homoerotic that song was. And, as that epiphany hit me, suddenly the dream shifted to brilliant color and all of the dancers I'd been watching all night at Union Jack's came out and backed Elvis up—all gloriously naked. Salome was fronting them as they did the bump and grind like their lives depended on it—all the hips in perfect unison with the young rocker.

Suddenly Steve came lurching though the throng of thong-less hotties. He, thankfully, was not naked, but a slash in his neck gaped widely open and his shirt was drenched in blood. A wet, dead and bedraggled Celeste rode on his shoulders, her red panties rubbing the back of his neck.

Jailhouse Rock played on and on until I woke up, sweaty and disoriented.

It was very early but I really didn't want to go back to sleep. I was packed and out of there. Half an hour later, I got a container of coffee, filled my cooler with beer, put the top down on the Impala and I-5 was taking me north.

...

EPILOGUE

Four pleasant hours later, I topped the hill south of Seattle to catch a panoramic view of downtown and Pioneer Square. I took the James Street exit, rolling down the hill to Second Avenue. Left turn and down to Yesler, the original Skid Row, and then down First South to the Central Saloon.

I parked the Impala in the commercial loading zone—hey, it ain't registered in my name—put on my best limping, lopsided swagger and pushed the door open. I was home again.

Several of the usual suspects were on their usual barstools and Monica was working the bar.

"Hey, Sailor, glad to have you back in town. The rumors have been flying about your exploits and we've got way too many PBRs back here," she said, and proved it by sliding one in front of me. She then introduced me to the other toothsome bar wench, another blonde with rather prominent cleavage. "This young lady, with the nice rack, is named Bob. This is Angus, our favorite resident pervert." Bob shook my hand and when she noticed where my wandering eyes wandered to, gave me a wry smile. All seemed to be well at my favorite watering hole.

I heard the door open behind me and several sets of eyes turned toward the door. An air of expectancy seemed to enter the venerable bar, along with whoever had just walked in. So I turned to find out what the big deal was about this particular barfly.

Kate Hickok stood in the doorway with a big grin on her tan and beautiful face. She slid onto the stool next to me and gave me a couple of pats on the butt.

"Glad to see you made it back in one piece... and in a week or so instead of ten-to-twenty," she smiled.

I nodded. "With some help from a good lawyer and a local Dowager Queen, who wishes you love and her best."

Kate suddenly looked very solemn.

"Yeah. I'm going down to visit that good lady real soon. I may not be going to get too many more chances to get to know her, and I want to. I don't want to lose her and Daddy before I get to know her—and not just to blow smoke up her ass because she might leave me a lot more money when she dies. Shit, I got a lot of money now." She made a wry face and chuckled.

"A year ago I was dead broke and bankrupt, working in a peep show, showing my cunt to anybody who wanted to see it and had a quarter. Now I'm a woman of property, an employer of note, being courted by the Chamber of Commerce. Life sure can be a kick in the ass."

That was quite a speech and for once, I just shut up and tried to look thoughtful. "Well," I finally said, "my bank account is fat enough that I won't have to deal with any crazy or sketchy people for a long time."

She nodded and narrowed her eyes.

"Yes, I give you about forty-eight hours to get good and restless," she said. She handed me a piece of paper.

"Listen, please do me one last piece of work. Here's the name and phone number of the poor bastard who owns the Impala. He's pretty tore up about Amanda. I liked her a lot, and loved to eat her pussy, but I think he really loved her. I talked to him yesterday and I would really rather not do it again, so soon. So will you see that his car gets back to him? Rooby is parked right behind it. I had the best team of body and fender people and mechanics I could find go over her from stem to stern. No more bullet holes or torn upholstery... or flat tires. I even had the engine and tranny rebuilt. With a little luck, which you seem to have in abundance on a good day..." (here I knocked on the bar) "... you should be driving her for a good long time."

"Thanks for everything, I'm glad you survived. I'll get it back to him," I said.

She grinned. "And through the whole thing I never had to turn a trick for money. I love stripping and I'm having a stripper's pole installed in my condo. I know a lady who gives lessons. She's amazing. But I just don't think I'd make a very good whore," she shook her head. "I didn't think there's anything wrong with it. It's almost a public service. Lonely men need sex too, but I just think I like being a talented amateur and something of a professional wanker. So you take good care of yourself and I'll see you around the Square. I'll have you over for a fancy meal before too long. I'm as good a cook as I am a stripper." She hugged me and kissed me and walked out of the bar.

I nodded, grabbed an *Underground* magazine, and got back to my beer.

Seattle, July 22, 2008

About Angus Vieira

The Judicial System where he was raised seemed to take a dim view of Angus' beer drinking and driving habits when he was eighteen years old and persuaded him that his natural talents would be better utilized flying around hugging a machine gun in Med-Evac choppers for the Marines in a far country he had never heard of with a bunch of other refocused juvenile delinquents.

This actually worked out for him better than he probably deserved since he lived through it and acquired a love of world travel only surpassed by his personal dislike of wearing uniforms.

He solved this by lucking into an entry level job in the engine department of a far sailing scientific research vessel that took him around the world the first of many times as he climbed through the ranks of the American Flag Merchant Marines. He served on vessels of all types from super tankers and container ships to coastwise freighters and oceanographic research ships that were his personal favorites.

When he was on dry land he could usually be seen driving across North America in a convertible and driving a cab around his native Seattle before deregulation wrecked that business.

But where ever he was, you would find a book close beside him.

He is the author of one book of poetry, The Snake Swallower of Cochin and Other

Odd Occupations—Published by Year of the Dragon Press 1995.

He has loved mystery books since he read his first Hardy Boys when he was eleven years old. This is his first try at that venerable art form.

These days he follows the sun in a mobile home from one clothing optional resort to another writing books and occasionally dancing around naked.

■■■

THE AUTHOR

ANGUS VIEIRA

PHOTO BY KATE WYATT

MURDER ON A SMALL ISLAND

By

ANGUS VIEIRA

A sneak Peek **At The Next Tale Of Mayhem And Murder In The On Going Adventures Of Angus Vieira**

Prologue

Bill Brownwen, Homicide Sergeant assigned to Seattle's East Precinct, stood staring down at the kneeling bronze statue of Jimi Hendrix. Jimi had his head thrown back in mid scream as he chorded his bronze guitar. The thrown back head and frozen scream brought Sergeant Bill back to the dead man in the alley, one hundred feet away down East Pine Street—the dead man that brought him out here to smoke his first cigarette in six months.

A short slender oriental lady came up to stand next to him and follow his gaze down at the guitar player. Detective Tina Lo had been his partner for over five years. They had what seemed an almost psychic way of communicating. She glanced at the smoke in his hand and decided not to bust his balls about sliding back into a habit he had fought hard to lose.

"They want to get the 'vic' downtown. You need another look?" She asked.

He shook his head and said, "I'd kind of like to stop looking at him inside my head. You hungry? My favorite pizza joint is just across the street."

She turned and gave a thumb jerk at the uniform at the head of the alley. He nodded and walked back into the alley. "Sure, I could use a better smell in my nose."

They left Jimi kneeling there and walked across Broadway to the corner of the Seattle Central Community College campus and then jaywalked across Pine, past the Theater to the corner bar restaurant named Bill's Off Broadway. They went in and turned up the steps and walked back to a small window table. The tattooed and pierced college student-waitress came quickly to take their order. A medium Bill's Special and a coke for her and a pint of local amber ale for Sergeant Brownwen.

Again she refrained from giving his nuts a small squeeze about the beer. They caught the case around five in the morning and it was now noon with no end of the shift in sight.

He got out his notebook. She did too. He went first.

"Okay. White male killed somewhere else and dropped in the alley, just two blocks from the East Precinct. So, we got a 'perp' with a set of balls."

"The victim was tall, maybe six three, Caucasian, brown hair, no eye color..." He looked up from his notebook, "...because the sick asshole took his eyes out." Brownwen glanced back down at his notes, "He also twisted his feet so far that ankle bones were sticking out like cactus spines. Either before or after which he smashed his knees and crushed his testicles. Doc is real certain all of that happened before he stabbed something deep in his asshole and waited while he bled out before loading him in some kind of vehicle, my bet being a pickup with a bed you can easily hose out."

Brownwen stopped as the waitress brought his beer and her coke. He took a deep drink. Lo nodded and took over.

"He also hammered his mouth and took something like a butane torch to his hands, so it's going to be a while before we find out who he was, if we ever do." She shook her head. "Let alone who did it."

The deep dish pizza arrived with the cheese still bubbling. It smelled delicious.

. . .

CHAPTER ONE

I had been back from Nevada about six weeks. It was a lovely August afternoon in Pioneer Square and I was in one of my favorite spots in the world. It was a round aluminum table with a big umbrella over it in a tiny courtyard in front of the Central Saloon.

I have a theory, of course because I have a line of shit approximately a mile long, it goes something like this, I really believe, well at least part of the time, that there are some places on earth that have a sort of important quality that's almost magic. You could call these places or points Nexuses if you wanted to. And everyone, currently alive, who has some kind of historic significance, will walk past that spot at some point-in-time... a phrase I hate and continue to use. Any way, First Avenue South is one such place.

Or maybe I should slow down on the Pabst Blue Ribbon in the afternoon.

Not that that is likely to happen.

My Cobra headed sword cane was lying across the table next to my beer and I picked it up and twirled it thinking again about the time it saved my life by not stabbing someone. I put it down and decided I should have another beer while I waited for Jesus and "Aunti-Jesus" to saunter down the street to share a pitcher and grab a couple of Cheddar Cheese Burgers with a side of fries, or a stripper on sabbatical from Las Vegas, wearing a short skirt with no underpants, to sit down across from me and wink, or whatever would liven up my afternoon; when my cell phone started chirping.

I had no idea how interesting my life was about to get.

It was a very familiar number.

"Hi Deario," I said. "How's the financial empire biz these days?"

Kate Hickok and I went back a ways. Since we had returned from Nevada we did brunch once a week on Sunday mornings. Ironically this was something she used to do with her father while he was still alive, but it was good for both of us. We had somehow become family. One night when we both had several PBRs she told me she thought of me as a cross between a Grandfather and a brother.

"Angus, you have got to come up to the office right away. I just thought up a job for you that is right up your dirty little alley."

"Kate, my little Honey Bucket, you know how my knee hates stairs these days. Come down here and I'll buy you a beer and a bowl of Chili, that'll give you enough gas to get to Pittsburg."

She put on a really terrible Bogart accent. I know that because mine is bad and hers is a lot worse.

"No way Slim, this is a private matter for a confidential gumshoe. At the Central Saloon even the toilet paper dispensers have ears."

She was probably right. Someone once said that Seattle is a collection of seven villages packed very closely together. Well, Pioneer Square is a special little village all on its own and gossip and beer have an old love affair.

"Okay," I sighed in a put-upon voice, "I'll race right over there. But that means you're buying the beer."

Monica, the lovely bartender came out to see what my bottle level looked like.

I shook my head sadly.

"Keep my tab going sweetheart, I have been summoned by the Cinderella of strippers."

She laughed and patted my ass as she went back inside. She knew I'd be right back. The place is my second living room.

I sauntered up the street. Actually my right knee is getting better every day thanks to tough Norwegian genes and Ibuprofen. I was just more comfortable watching the bouncy ass walking up the street.

The Pioneer Building sits like a regal small fortress on the corner of First Avenue and the termination of the steep hill that is Cherry Street. It's at least a hundred and twenty years old but beautifully maintained. It houses mostly criminal lawyers and accountants, but it's also the home of Hickok Enterprises, a small empire of strip clubs, bars and apartment buildings owned and run quite well by Kate since the quick and violent demise of her father.

I stopped in the cobblestone triangular square in front of the building long enough to touch the bronze statue of Chief Sealth for luck. 'Maybe next time you will spend less time living in harmony with nature and invent gunpowder,' I thought. There is a lesson there somewhere. I glanced up at the windows wrapping around the corner of the second floor and winked.

That was Kate's office suite. I saw her glance down and wave.

Usually I take the wide sweeping staircase, but in deference to my knee I got in a shiny brass fitted elevator and floated gently upward. The wrought iron doors opened in the hallway outside her office and I walked in and stopped dead as I got a massive hit of Deju Vu all over again, as Yogi used to say.

Across the small room, a young woman was bending over a three drawer filing cabinet next to a secretary desk, going through the files. Well I assumed she was young but she was certainly a woman wearing a very short skirt that did little to cover a lovely ass clad in extremely tight bright red panties with a fetching camel toe.

It took me right back to the first time I came in this room several months ago. The owner of that butt had sent me on the way to Nevada. My right knee gave me a sudden bright second of pain. Then I heard a peal of Kate's distinctive hearty laughter from the next room and the owner of this set of fetching cheeks stood up with a giggle, which sent some interesting ripples through her rear end.

It took me a long half a minute to lose my irritation and see that the joke was on me, and it was a very effective one. I strode by the pretty petite strawberry blonde who was grinning up at me, giving her ass a loud spank as I entered Kate's corner office shaking my head.

"You have got to be having a real slow day here in Nookie Central if all you have to do is annoy the shit out of your favorite P.I."

"Ah come on Angie, you losing your sense of humor and becoming an adult. You need any help getting rid of that panty wad you got going?" She pouted for about a second and then went back to grinning as the slender blonde in the scarlet drawers came in after me and tripped around the desk to plop down on her lap.

Kate gave her a kiss on the cheek and copped a feel of her pert right breast.

"This is Tanya, Tanya this is Angus, he is a dirty, dirty unrepentant pervert that you can trust with your life if he is your friend." She gave Tanya a spank that made her jump up rubbing her ass and come around the desk to sit on my lap and stick her tongue out at Kate making a short farting noise.

"I like him already." She kissed my cheek and stroked my neck. "You'll be my friend won't you?"

"I can't wait." I said sincerely.

Kate slapped the desk with a mock frown.

"All right you two. Get a room!" She barked.

"I've got a room," I murmured. "In a nice sleazy motel on Aurora Avenue North."

"Mmmmmmmm, my kind of man." Tanya said, wiggling her butt around, which caught the attention of my trouser snake.

Kate shook her head at my smile. "Hey, over here Horatio Horndog. I've got a potentially serious pain in the ass coming my way."

"Believe me, so does Tanya." I countered.

Tanya punched me on the arm, but she smirked while she did. She stood up adjusting her skirt, or wide belt, which would be a better description, and perched on the corner of Kate's desk, still giving me a distracting flash of scarlet occasionally.

"Okay, I'll be an adult for a while. What is it exactly that has your knickers in a twist?" I tried to remember where I left my serious face.

Kate put her hands on the desk and frowned at me. "You don't have to try to be an adult, I don't want you to strain to hard and hurt yourself. This job, like the last one you did just demands the skills you possess."

"And those are?" I said, shamelessly fishing for a compliment.

"Those of an energetic juvenal delinquent, with an unusual lack of compunctions," She shot back.

I nodded, thinking about it. I guess a compliment from Ms. Hickok was a little much to hope for. She knew me too well.

"Okay, you have discovered the key to my talents and skill set. So what can this refugee from the road company of West Side Story do for you?"

"First liar hasn't got a chance—I've heard you sing, and seen you dance." She grimaced.

"Anyway, here's what's wrong with my little stripper empire. Two words. Donald Dimes."

"Okay," I thought for a moment, "He is a fat politician with a really big head. I didn't realize you had developed such an active sense of civic responsibility. Is this Kate the King Maker talking?"

"This could seriously effect the lives and livelihoods of a whole bunch of very talented young women with advanced interpersonal entertainment skills, and very little in the way of modesty." She said with a frown, but then smirked. You have to smirk after a sentence like that.

"Wow," I shook my head in admiration. "Those Shoreline Community College remedial English courses have really started to kick in. How, exactly, is Mr. Dimes menacing the multi-skilled sluts who are your independent contractors?"

"Dummy Dimes, if I can give him a nickname I hope will catch on, has decided that Seattle's strippers' moral fiber is not to be trusted within four feet of the paying customers in my clubs. Why is it that so many sexually frustrated, middle aged men and women, too, for some inextricable reason, feel the need to protect society from sexual contact?" She looked at me like she really expected me to explain it to her. I shrugged and gave her my bemused look.

Obviously this had put a real burr under her saddle. She plunged on, "You know many of these girls a lot better than you deserve to. Do you want them to have to move to

Portland to make any money with their erotic exhibitionism? These ladies are raising kids and going to school to learn how to do something else when their tits start to sag. They are responsible and decorative citizens. They are not doing this just to get heartfelt compliments from some jerkoid in the front row with his hands in his lap."

I was trying to think up a proper or improper response to this when something nudged my ankle and I looked down to see a small brown furry head sniffing my right sock. Something even I do as seldom as possible.

"Kate, don't panic when I tell you this. There is a large rodent under your desk. Hand me your stapler."

I stuck my hand out and she slapped it, hard.

"That's NOT A RODENT you oaf. That is a wonderful lagomorph named Carmichael and if you hurt a single hair on his furry bunny head you will go right to the head of my permanent shit list."

Kate jumped up and came quickly around the desk and gently picked the rabbit up. He, I assumed it was a he with that name, had really long ears and kind of a tawny golden brown fur. Kate held him in her arms across her chest on his back like you would a newborn baby, stroking and rubbing his ears. A look that I can only describe as bunny bliss washed over his face. Carmichael's rear leg started kicking vigorously, massaging Kate's right tit.

"He loves this almost as much as he loves his daily portion of banana." She said.

"I never had much to do with rabbits, but I figured that one out." I said.

Tanya joined in rubbing the rabbit's belly. I might have been suffering a slight case of Bunny envy.

"Iago whatsit?" I asked.

"A lagomorph is a plant eating animal with two sets of upper jaw incisors for munching Kale. Isn't it bun bun." She set him down on her desk day planner where he promptly excreted a couple of pellets of shit and pissed on the paper.

"Bun Bun, what am I going to do with you?" She scolded and scooped him back up and deposited him in a plastic dish tub partially filled with straw. He looked completely unrepentant chewing on a piece of straw. "He's a lean mean pooping machine."

I took another long look. No, the rabbit wasn't white and he did not have a pocket watch.

It was a little strange reconciling this girl with the tough ass business lady I knew.

I decided to blow a little smoke up her pretty ass and change the subject. "Okay, this is a whole new side of you for me, but it just adds another dimension to your complex personality."

"Stop blowing smoke up my ass." She said tapping the desk. "You're not very good at it anyway. "Okay we'll get back to the devious Mr. Dimes."

"I want this dickhead decidedly discredited and disgraced and denounced and, and..."

"Dismembered?" I supplied.

"I'll help." Tanya chimed in.

I was trapped in a room with two lovely homicidal rabbit worshippers, 'and loving it' as Maxwell Smart might say.

"I'll tell you what. Let me start the discrediting and disgracing and you can look through your daddy's rolodex for the other options. I just bought these shoes. Why don't I see if I can find a beautiful woman to seduce this fat fuck in a certain motel room I know that has a one way mirror to the next unit. It's conveniently located on Aurora and for a healthy tip the owner operator is happy to help me out. It's gonna be kind of expensive though."

"I call it money well spent if it saves my clubs and these girl's livelihoods." She was very serious now.

"Okay then. I'll see if the lady I used last time is still around."

I pulled out my cell phone. Have I mentioned that my moral decisions are subject to situational modification?

Tanya came over and closed my phone up as she sat back down on my lap. "I said I wanted to help. Let's come up with a plan over dinner."

She turned away from me toward Kate. I can't be sure she winked.

"You want to come to dinner with us Boss?"

Boss lady shook her head with a small smile.

"No, no you kiddies run along and have fun."

Tanya jumped up and went to get her stuff and I leaned over the desk and quietly asked Kate, "So are you having sex with that young lady?"

She shook her head and grinned. "No. I make it a rule not to have sex with the staff. Which also means you and me by the way."

I grinned and shook my head, "Oh Kate, my friend, we are way beyond that." And I walked out.

■ ■ ■

CHAPTER TWO

Tanya skipped down the stairs to wait for me in the lobby. I tried to make it look like I was being dignified instead of just listening to the internal barking of my right knee.

I don't think I fooled her. She stood down there grinning. Then she glanced around to make sure we were alone and spun around, bent over to give me a Can Can ass shake in those red panties. I was really beginning to like this girl.

I goosed her. Deeply. "Where should I take your naughty butt to fill it up with food?" I asked.

"My, my, that's the sweetest dinner invitation I think I've ever received." She batted her eyes.

"That's the romantic poet, sensitive new age part of me oozing out all over you."

"Oh boy, you're really giving me an appetite. Lead on, I'll follow you anywhere." Then she goosed me. Deeply.

Once again I tried to look dignified, after a small yelp.

We sauntered south down First Avenue catching appreciative glances I had little or nothing to do with. Tanya was just as easy on the eyes as her fetching employer.

When we got to the Central Saloon she went right over to ROOBY, my car parked in front of the little patio and patted her fender.

"Your car... am I right?" I nodded. "Will you take me for a ride after we eat?"

ROOBY would be pissed at me if I didn't." I assured her. "Do you want to go someplace classy for dinner? Or eat right here at the Central?"

"I heard that." A voice cracked like a whip.

Oops. That was Monica's voice coming from behind me. I turned around and sure enough, there she was, hands on her hips frowning at me.

"This place is classy, well second classy anyway." She pointed to the sign painted in gold leaf on the window. 'Seattle's Oldest Second Class Saloon. Established 1892.'

Tanya came to my rescue.

"I love the food here! And we can sit out here on the patio and make fun of the strolling tourists. Hey,Mon." She ran over and gave Monica a big hug.

"Maybe Furious George has made some meatloaf and garlic mashed potatoes." I said hopefully. "And you can put a half carafe of your finest house red in a bucket of ice for me.

I know the thought of chilling a Merlot or a 'Cab' makes wine snobs sneer. Well fuck them. "I like my wine cold and my ladies hot," I said to Tanya and she winked at me and smiled.

"This is beginning to look like your lucky day." She said.

Monica brought me a Pabst blue Ribbon long neck and Tanya a Jack and Coke, without us even having to ask and we started to get acquainted.

"This party could get kind of rough you know? At the very least you will have to have an evening of sweaty sex with a fat would be politician, who might not have the worlds best hygiene, and all of it on camera." I told her wearing my very serious face.

She frowned and shrugged, then was quiet for a few minutes, thinking about it as she sipped her drink. I sipped my beer and let her make up her mind. If she was going to back out of this, I sure wouldn't blame her. And this would be the best time to do it. No hard feelings, except the one she was engendering in my pants.

Finally the frown left her face and she gave me a smile.

"Sorry about the dead air time. I was deciding how much I should tell you about me and how fucked up some parts of my life have been. I decided on letting pretty much all of it hang out. Hope I don't shock you."

I chuckled. "I'm kind of hard to shock."

"We'll see. First off, I owe Kate a lot for taking me out of the strip clubs and giving me this assistant gig. She even gave me a raise. I've got two kids that are living with my foster mom, so I can use it.

"My real Mom is piece of work. I haven't seen her in years. She was the first drugged out slut in my life. Some of my earliest memories are of her bringing her boyfriend into my room in the middle of the night so he could fondle me, her 'little girl,' while she blew him or fucked him. It was the way I was raised. I didn't even know that wasn't the way all families lived until I was six or seven and someone explained it to me after they took me away and put me in the first of a series of foster homes."

She stopped for a moment to get my reaction.

"Okay, I take it back about doubting that you could shock me." I managed to choke out.

I looked out at the sidewalk for a couple of minutes while I got my voice and my anger under control. The first trickle of families wearing blue 'T' shirts with a big silver S on the chests were marching by headed for Quest Field , stalwart Mariners fans with the vain hope that some miracle will get us a wild card spot in the play offs.

"I am a sexual activist. I think that pretty much anything that two consenting adults do with each other is their business. I happen to like women," I shrugged "but if two guys or two girls, or more want to rub around, well get it on. Several years ago I had a lady friend that liked orgies and we used to go to about one a month."

"But don't fuck the puppies! Let the kids get old enough to understand and make their own decision about sex. If you see a bunch of puppies rolling around on the carpet you don't think, Ah look at them, they're so cute I think I'll fuck one and fuck up its life forever. It's amazing you turned out to have as positive an attitude as you do."

She spent a couple of minutes watching the baseball fans walk by. Well looking at them with her mind way back in her past. She leaned over closer to me and lowered her voice.

"The first time I sucked a cock for money I was thirteen. Well it was for drugs which is the same thing. As soon as I turned eighteen I went to work for Kate's Daddy in his strip clubs. And yes, I fucked him more than once."

"He always treated me good as far as I can see. I made money for him yes, but I made a lot of money for me, too. He gave me a safe and protected place to work my trade and meet my clients. It was a good working system, but I've been at it for going on ten years. I'm really getting stripper burn out. I've gotten all the drugs out of my life except for booze and a little pot. When Kate took over the clubs after her daddy died so horribly I was ready for a change. I opened up to her. She understands better than he ever could because she's been up there on that stage being looked at like a piece of yummy meat."

She stopped to take a drink.

"Okay I get it. If you have to have sex with a fat slob, you are not only not in love with but don't even like, it won't be the first time. Even if the cameras are running."

She nodded and grinned. "And I'll be the savior of the jobs of all the strippers in King County. I'll get all the pussy I could ever need."

She lasciviously licked her lips.

"You, young lady are enthusiastically erotic. I like that in a girl. You know, I might not be able to keep this little epic off the internet. It will be Kate's call. As a matter of fact flooding the net with his big ass might be the final blow to his career."

She shrugged again.

"I'll change my hair color and try to give him all the face time. I'll just keep my face under his over hanging belly." She laughed loud and long and after a second I joined in. We were still staring at each other chuckling when Monica arrived with the dinners and a carafe of chilled Merlot. You can spend a lot more money for a couple of dinners in downtown Seattle and not have nearly as good a meal.

"If you two are making a movie I'll buy a copy."

"Oh, you'll get to see it I promise. It's gonna be a real crowd pisser." I promised.

After dinner I gave her the top down convertible ride she wanted. We drove up Western Avenue under and then past the Pike Street Market to my favorite freeway entrance.

You go up a ramp off Western Avenue to a yield sign right at the entrance to the south end of the Battery Street Tunnel and wait for a gap in the north bound traffic coming up The Alaskan Way Viaduct and then you stomp on the gas shooting up the tunnel which always reminds me the beginning of the old Sci-fi channel series Sliders.

Tanya whooped and screamed sending echoes bouncing off the walls.

The politicians keep hammering away that the Alaskan Way Viaduct is going to fall down the next time one of our geological faults fart. This is a large steaming pile of bullshit I my humble opinion. I think some of Seattle's super rich movers and shakers are salivating to get at the waterfront property that tearing it down would open up. They never commute anywhere. It's one of my all time favorite roads.

Tanya scooted over next to me so I put my arm around her. She had her head thrown back with her hair blowing in the wind. Her left hand started slowly rubbing the crotch of my five-oh-ones—a small smile on her lips. My right hand might have touched her right nipple once or twice. She was not wearing a bra, nor did she need to. Yes that might have happened once or twice.

Somewhere around the eight thousand block of Aurora Avenue North I pulled into the parking lot of a fairly large motel complex stopping in front of the office. Ali Dinn looked out the window waving vigorously.

Ali Dinn is a Sikh. A member of the tall, proud Hindu people that I've always thought had as much to do with the British keeping control of their Indian Empire as the Enfield rifle and the stalwart English underclass troopers that Rudyard Kipling depicted in Soldiers Three, several volumes of Barracks Room Ballads and the stirring poem, Gunga Din. Kipling has somehow acquired the reputation as a racist. Mostly from people who must not have read him I suspect. Probably the same people who want to ban Huckleberry Finn.

I have often wanted to ask Mr. Dinn if Gunga was an ancestor, but I never have. Mr. Dinn's personality has a few sharp edges. A lot of my friends do, come to think of it. Some people think I have myself.

Anyway I trust this man. He can keep a secret as well as anyone I've ever met in my life. I would hate to have the job of getting him to tell something he had been told in confidence. That's in spite of the fact he seems to spend most of the day on the phone with his relatives.

I went in, shook his hand and we caught up on a few mutual acquaintances. Most of them cab drivers. He was drinking a mug of some kind of fragrant tea. He asked if he could get me or my companion some, glancing briefly at Tanya as she smiled and waved through the window. I declined for both of us.

Behind the counter, Incense burned in front of a statue of Ganesha playing the flute. It was about two feet tall and made of well polished brass. I always compliment him on this. Ganesha is by far my favorite Hindu God. The Lord of Success, God of Wisdom and Wealth was, for my Theosophical buck, the go to God.

I was sure Mr. Dinn had a pretty good idea why I was there, but we have to get through some polite conversation to get around to it.

"I've got another godless infidel that needs to be taught a lesson Sir." I finally got around to mentioning.

"Well Sahib," he said, I know he calls me that every so often just to squeeze my nuts. "If you're going to teach all the godless infidels a lesson one at a time you are going to need those rooms for a long time."

"This one is special. I can let most of them slide for a while. Besides that I like it better when I get someone to sponsor my worthwhile social endeavors."

He nodded gravely. "You sometimes make Mother Teresa seem to be just another street slut."

He handed me two room keys with consecutive numbers in the back corner of the parking lot—ground floor.

"Same price as always." He said.

I nodded. "Fine, my sponsor has some very deep pockets and an abiding deep dislike for this particular asshole. I don't know how long it will take to teach him this particular life changing lesson."

"The mill wheels of Karma sometimes grind slowly." He said gravely.

"I think you just seriously mixed your metaphysical metaphors." I said just as gravely as I walked back out to the car where Tanya was waiting patiently.

I started the car and moved it to park in the furthest corner of the lot.

"Let me show you your palatial new crib baby." I threw an arm around her shoulders as I worked the lock on the last door on this floor. Room sixty-nine. "I don't think the number is entirely coincidental."

"Mmmmm yummy." She murmured.

It was a fairly normal mid-market motel room with a king size bed, big television with the remote laying on one of the four pillows. There were some interesting touches that elevated it, or lowered it depending on your point of view to the realm of a two hour fuck gymnasium. There was an eight foot, round mirror on the ceiling over the bed and another eight foot long oval mirror on the wall behind the head of the bed both reflecting the emerald green satin bed spread. The carpet was white shag that looked like it should live in fear of the first sloppy drunk with a bottle of red wine.

The night stands at each side of the bed each held a large round ashtray with a mirrored bottom and two goose necked lamps—one with a bright white light bulb, the other one, bright red.

Tanya stood for a while with her arms folder across her chest. Then she turned to me with a mock serious expression and said, "There is a subtle theme to this ambiance I can't quite put my middle finger on."

She gave a great belly laugh and through herself on the bed with her legs pointed to the ceiling so she could admire the crotch of her red panties. I kissed my fingers and gave the aforementioned spot a brisk friendly rub as I said, "You have some fun here while I check the room next door."

I left her with her arms bracing her body on the bed as she did some amazing vertical splits.

I went back out the door, walking down the covered walkway; which was intentionally shadowed without the lights that usually illuminate motel walkways, and used my key to room sixty-eight.

Like the other room, this one had a king size bed to the left against the wall. This one, with a more normal beige bedspread and the carpet was a darker brown—short and tough. The kind that would laugh at red wine. Against the wall that connected this room to Tanya's, there were two desks that took up most of the wall all the way back to the vanity alcove outside the bathroom door. One held a cabinet that had the requisite big television. The other desk was backed by a mirror that went up to about a foot from the ceiling. There in lay the feature that made these two rooms rent for a hundred and a half a night each.

I shut the light switch by the door off and small dim red lights came on in the four upper corners of the room. I walked over and sat down at the desk, feeling around under the drawer till I found the remembered button and pushed it. The mirrors slide silently sideways into the wall.

Tanya was sitting about three feet in front of me, seemingly completely unaware of the fact that a voyeur with very few moral scruples was watching her every move. She had a small pipe in her hand, glass with white and purple swirls all over it. She took another hit, held it in for a long time and then blew it at her reflection on the ceiling. I don't think she was smoking Edward G. Robinson pipe tobacco.

She continued to gaze at the mirror on the ceiling with a vague smile on her face. Her right hand raised her tiny semblance of a skirt. She idly start scratch her scarlet crotch. Then she put the pipe on the bed beside her and flipped backward onto her shoulders with her arms forming triangles with her hands on the back of her ribcage.

Her left hand whipped her panties up her legs over her high heels, really high heels at the moment, and threw them at the ceiling with a loud whoop of laughter. Her fingers got very busy sliding around her pink lipped jade pagoda while her small puckered asshole winked at me.

I watched her for a few minutes thoroughly enjoying the show with nary a trace of guilt. There was not a single chance in hell she didn't know she was putting on a private show just for me. I didn't know if she ever worked at the Lusty Lady, but she knew her way around a small bed shaped stage. She could sell a masturbation show the way Bruce Springsteen sells a song.

Eventually I closed the silent sliding doors, stood up and walked out the door, locking it behind me. If there had been a box for it she would have been fifty dollars richer.

I walked in the door of her room. She was grinning at me.

"Did I do a good audition? Do I get the part?" She asked innocently.

I walked over to the bed and gently took a buttock in each hand and kissed her right on the tip of her girlish trigger.

I unbuttoned my five-o-ones.
"You are about to receive your Oscar."

...

Stay Tuned For The Rest Of The Story.

www.ingramcontent.com/pod-product-compliance
Lightning Source LLC
Chambersburg PA
CBHW022001010726
47494CB00003B/842